PLACE OF TORMENT

MAYA DANIELS

BOOKS

By Maya Daniels

Infernal Regions for the Unprepared

Black Hand

Lower World

Everlasting Fire

Place of Torment

By N Gray

The Dana Mulder Suspense Thriller Series

Deadly Pattern

Devil Mountain

Chasing Evil

Nightcrawler

Vinci Books

vinci-books.com

Published by Vinci Books Ltd in 2025

1

The publisher and the author have made every effort to obtain permissions for any third party material used in this book and to comply with copyright law. Any queries in this respect should be brought to the attention of the publisher and any omissions will be corrected in future editions.

A CIP catalogue record for this book is available from the British Library.

Paperback ISBN: 9781036701772

Chapter One

THE HARD CONCRETE beneath my bruised body was awful. When I tried to move onto my side, my hips digging into the ground was not pleasant. I gave up on trying to get comfortable and rolled onto my back even though my spine and shoulders ached.

As to what had happened—*he did*. As much as I wanted to forget everything—*I couldn't*. The memories were still fresh in my mind, like a bitter pill I kept choking on.

My tongue stuck to my palate when I swallowed, and I craved an ice-cold glass of water. Slowly I sat up. My surroundings were dark and unknown. There were iron bars for walls, with the night sky for a ceiling. Behind me was a large house at least three stories high made mostly from glass than brick or wood. The second story had a large balcony, and when I rocked onto my tiptoes, I could discern a bar area to the side with the doors wide open. Someone was home and had left me *here*—in a freakin' cage like one would keep a large animal. In front of me was a yard of sorts; I wasn't quite sure what kind of yard, but it was large.

I couldn't tell where the wall began and the trees ended it was so vast. I mostly saw shadows and outlines of trees, with another building in the distance.

My cage contained no luxuries. The floor was concrete with dark spots I could only assume was body fluids from those before me. I imagined the state those poor people had been in when they were brought here, awaiting their ultimate demise—their bodies bruised and their minds broken. It wasn't the law that had brought them here or any medieval knight but six people who lived the vigilante lifestyle, but instead of bringing the guilty to justice, they held their own court where the person was only guilty in *their* eyes. Handing down a death sentence to all by way of a sport; with the wide-open spaces, I imagined the person running for their life with nowhere to go. Only the fastest could survive for long, but the ultimate price was with their life. I supposed the resulting end would be welcomed after spending time with those six.

Shivering, I hugged myself tighter. My teeth chattered when a wind caressed my skin as I looked for a way out of my situation. I flinched at the voice behind me.

"Dana …" His voice was so deep I could feel it in my bones. He exhaled. "My god, you were hard to catch." Before, he'd always worn a mask, which distorted his voice, but now, I could hear the real him, and I knew who *he* was —I could recognize that voice anywhere.

I turned in his direction and rubbed my arms for warmth. "You!"

Chapter Two

THREE DAYS AGO...

Wednesday

I SIPPED my coffee while my laptop switched on. Marc was in the kitchen, fetching a cup of the delicious black liquid I had made. Nigel was still missing after five days. Marc and I had split up and visited all the various hospitals, police stations, and morgues, showing staff pictures of our colleague, our friend, but he wasn't there. He wasn't injured, arrested, or dead. He was just *gone*—vanished into thin air.

Marc knew of family members Nigel had back West, but they hadn't heard from him since a mass murderer, Carl Bingham, had massacred his family during a robbery in an ice cream parlor near Devil Mountain while his brother Kevin drove the getaway vehicle. The two had escaped capture for over fifteen years until recently.

I had received information on the ice cream parlor and what had happened years ago on the same day Nigel had received an anonymous letter, detailing Carl's name, address, and a recent photo. We had found this letter in his desk drawer while we were busy searching for anything on why or where he had disappeared to. Nigel had driven back to Devil Mountain to fetch the police report for me, but he didn't stay there nor did he come home. Instead, Nigel had sent Billie photos of the report instead of dropping the copied files with me. Then he had gone after Carl himself. Nigel had found Carl and butchered him—tied his wrists and stretched him out in the center of the ice cream parlor, cut up his abdomen and watched him bleed to death. Then Nigel had disappeared.

For five days, we had been searching and still nothing.

I continued with my case load while Marc did the same. Neither of us wanted to say the obvious, to say what we thought—that Travis and his vigilante killers had gotten hold of Nigel. The killers got *rid* of him like they had so many others before him.

It was a vicious circle; revenge killings never ended. Someone would always get hurt—someone left alone once they had lost a loved one. This madness wouldn't end until we stopped it. I wasn't sure how this would be done, but we needed to find Travis and the rest of his group and either kill them ourselves or try turn them over to the police. The problem was they were a hard bunch to find, and we had no idea who the rest were. I suspected Aika, the exotic-looking assistant at Seekster, was one of them. The types of questions she'd asked me and then stared in my direction were obvious clues she was involved in more ways than just as an assistant to Travis, but it was hard to prove.

We needed to get our hands on a few things: proof of who they were, proof of their involvement in any of the murders, and their dealings with Travis, along with signed statements. But there were no bodies, no eyewitnesses, and no proof. I was toying with the idea of gaining Aika's trust and getting information from her, but I had no idea how far she was into Travis's game or if there was a way to bring her in. Johnny and I had spoken extensively about this, and he was trying to do things on his side with the FBI, but nothing had been agreed upon yet, so it was up to us to do *something*.

My laptop chimed continuously as the emails loaded one after the other. None of the emails were about Nigel, so I sat back and finished my cup of coffee first before I answered them.

The doorbell chimed when a delivery guy entered with a package. He scanned the clipboard in one hand and checked the address on the package then stopped before my desk. "Are you Dana?"

"Yep." I stood to receive the package.

"Sign here please." The delivery guy handed me the clipboard.

I did as requested and swapped it for the package.

"Here you go."

Once he had left, I used my scissors to cut one side open.

"What's this?" Marc asked over my shoulder.

"I don't know." I arched an eyebrow. "I can guess who it's from though, and I won't lie, I'm a little afraid to know what's inside."

"Do you want me to do it?" Marc placed his mug on my desk and reached for the scissors in my grasp.

"Sure," I said, handing them over.

Marc cut away the tape, placed the scissors on the table and lifted the lid from inside the packaging. He dug both hands inside and removed a vase. "There's an inscription."

Marc read it to himself first then handed me the vase. "Now we know where Nigel is."

"What?" I asked, understanding what he'd said but not registering. The vase was a midnight marble blue with a silver lid. On the side was an inscription beautifully hand-crafted in calligraphy: *Here lies Nigel, Father, Husband, Friend.* I opened the lid to ensure and saw ashes; whether it was Nigel's was up for debate.

"They really did get to him."

"Of course, they did. They sent him information about his family's deaths, and he did what most would do—he went after the guy responsible for taking them away. They did this to lure him out on his own. Then Travis could catch him for himself and did who knows what to him." I returned the vase into the packaging and grabbed my mug with shaky hands.

"From what we've seen before, it wouldn't have been pretty."

I'd seen the photos of how Travis and his group tortured and maimed their victims, and it wasn't pleasant. Their imagination was scary, with the tools they had at their disposal.

"What are your plans for today?" Marc asked, changing the subject. He obviously didn't want to dwell on our discovery or the pain Nigel must've endured at Travis's hands, and neither did I. But that didn't mean I was about to sweep it under the carpet; we would figure out something and soon.

I placed my mug on the table and clicked on my calendar. "I have a nine o'clock. I'm handing over evidence to my client, then I'm out for the rest of the day."

"Okay, and you're only doing surveillance, Dana," Marc

chastised without me even doing anything wrong. "I don't want any hero stuff." He arched an eyebrow.

"I know, but just so you understand, if I'm attacked first, I will protect myself."

"I know." He averted his eyes and clicked something on his screen. "We are building evidence to take through the proper channels. We can't have you running around like a cowgirl, getting up to no good. And just because Travis isn't after you, at this moment, doesn't mean he isn't watching you."

I understood all too well what was at stake, because it wasn't just about revenge or stopping a bunch of killers; this was about justice and putting all of them behind bars. This was about their victims, no matter how bad they might have thought they were. What they had done was wrong and needed to be brought in—all of them.

My nine o'clock entered. I handed her the photos of her boyfriend, and she was not pleased, as expected. He'd professed his love to her, but he was also a gold digger. He had other girlfriends, other wealthy girlfriends, and once I'd contacted the others to let them know who they were dating, they all dumped him. And my client would be the next one to do the same.

After my client left, I packed my laptop, greeted Marc while he was on the phone and left the office. The drive to Seekster was forty minutes in traffic. Once I arrived, I found a parking spot across the street from the monstrous building and waited. I answered emails on my laptop, and by eleven, I packed it away, sat up straight and fastened my seatbelt. I noticed the raven hair before I saw her face.

Aika exited the secure building, crossed the street and into a parking garage. She didn't park underground of the building she worked in; instead, she parked across the street.

It was strategic for her to do so; it was a way for her to come and go undetected. The garage she used did not have any cameras nor did it have a person collecting the money. She paid for her ticket at the machine, climbed into her car and left; nobody saw her come and go—no witnesses to her actions. Except me.

I pulled from my parking spot and followed her bright red Mustang. We drove for about twenty minutes until she pulled into the driveway of a home in Winnetka. This was not her place; she lived in Oak Brook. Every day at this time, she stopped at this same address. I had no idea who lived here, but I would change that today even if I had to jump over a fence to see inside. The last three days, I'd been following Aika to get a feel for her routine and to see where she lived. I now had her home address—which was very different to her driver's license—and I knew what she preferred to eat for dinner. Sometimes the job was boring and mundane, but I had to do this; I had to learn more about this group and try to put a stop to them.

At first, Marc did not want me doing this, to follow her, but she was all we had. We did not have an address for Travis, and we didn't know who the others were. I'd first told Marc about the feeling she had given me when we were at Seekster and the types of questions she had asked and how she had said them to try to convince me she was involved with Travis in more ways than one. Only then did Marc agree that I keep an eye on her but only at a distance, and if I kept my current cases up to date.

I circled the block and stopped around the corner where she couldn't see me nor could the person who lived in that house from their second-floor window.

After two hours, Aika exited and drove past. The last few days I'd tailed her, she went straight back to the office.

Today, curiosity was gnawing at me, and I wanted to see for myself who lived in that house.

I climbed from my car and circled the block. Only one row of houses comprised the large block, and the target house sat between two other houses. Instead of going in front of the houses, I came around the back, hoping to see something—anything. The walls of that house were about six feet high and without a back gate. The house on the left had a gate, and the walls were lower; the house on the right didn't have a back gate either. I tested the handle on the gate for the left-side house, and it opened.

I waited to hear barking after the gate had clicked open, but when no attack dog appeared to maul me to death, I knew it was safe for me to enter. The back yard was large, and the house was quiet. The windows were devoid of curtains, and I couldn't see any furniture. From the emptiness of the house, I surmised it was unoccupied. I closed the gate behind me and followed the path to the house. When I reached the porch, I could see into the mysterious yard. A large pool sat behind a house made mostly from large glass panels that reflected light, and I couldn't see in.

As I was about to descend the stairs, movement caught my eye. Someone had closed the sliding door. Perhaps they were leaving. I needed to see who they were and where they were going. For Aika to come here every day must mean this person was important. It could be Travis or one of the others.

I ran down the stairs toward the gate. Once I reached my car, I climbed in and turned the key. A moment later, the black car drove past. I inched forward and saw the target house's gate close. That black car belonged to the owner of the house. I turned right and followed.

Chapter Three

THE BLACK MERCEDES-BENZ didn't have the usual license plate, only a unique, large *S*, and a fearful shudder ran through my body. This had to be Travis's car. It reminded me of what Kevin had said, the man who squatted at Devil Mountain and Calvin's brother. He had said he saw a man enter Devil Mountain near where he stayed and the car he drove was black with a large *S*. He didn't say where he saw the *S*, just that it was on the car.

The house Aika visited daily belonged to Travis. That thought alone set butterflies loose in my stomach. I knew where Pig-head lived. Yet, at the same time, an uneasy feeling settled where the butterflies flapped, and I didn't know what to do. It all fit into place; Travis was wealthy and had the means. His house was luxurious and expensive with the type of security system that would make a grown man cry with envy. I was positive that once you set foot inside there and you were unwelcome, you would not leave with a pulse.

I sent a text message to Marc with my location and what

I was doing just in case something happened to me. I snapped a picture of the sleek black car and sent that as well.

We drove for a while and passed Crystal Lake. At first, I thought he was heading to Woodstock, but he took a left turn onto a winding road, and my GPS lost signal. Smacking the device did not help, and I had to resort to my instincts and adjust to my surroundings. I'd never been here before and needed to concentrate on where he was going so I could find my way back out. I followed his car from a distance, then he disappeared. I slowed to a snail's pace and passed the exit he had taken. He drove along a dirt road and stopped near trees. I drove until I came to a T-junction and turned left, but he was still in view. When the road veered right, I turned around, hoping my movements weren't as obvious as they felt. I parked my car in a dip on the shoulder of the road so my car wasn't visible. When I climbed out, I couldn't see him; it was only when I crossed the road and walked up and into the grassy field could I lay eyes on him.

He was out of his car and walking toward something near tall trees. He wore dark clothing and had dark hair; from this distance, that's all I could discern. He crouched, and I continued watching but couldn't see what he was doing with his back to me. After about ten minutes, he returned to his car and drove the same way he had come.

I hurried across the street, climbed into my car and drove the road he had just left. I wanted to know what he had done and what was out here. After parking my car where he had, I ran the path toward the trees. Glancing to my right to the area where I had parked earlier, I couldn't see anything and knew he didn't see me—my car was in a ditch and out of sight. I sighed with relief, knowing he wasn't aware of me.

Ahead of me between the trees were two unmarked graves. Each stone had engraved patterns beautifully crafted with thought and care, and I knew they were significant. A person like Travis wouldn't come here for a friend; these were for two people he loved dearly—possibly his parents. Between the two stones lay a bouquet of fresh flowers in loose sand. I gathered he had dug up something or had buried something and placed the flowers on top to mask what he'd done. As much as I felt guilty for digging in the dirt near their graves, I wanted to know if he had buried something of importance here.

I dug into the sand until my fingertips hit something solid and cold—a metal box. I stood to ensure Travis hadn't turned around and returned. When I was sure I was still alone, I crouched again, pulled out the bouquet and placed it on top of one of the stones and scooped the loose sand with my hands. The box was large, and by the time I was done scooping, heaps of sand sat to one side. I couldn't pull it out, but I could open it. From the patterns on the lid, I ascertained it was an old 1970's breadbox. Inside the box was memorabilia—old photos, baby clothing, and a birth certificate. It felt like I'd hit the jackpot. I wanted to scream with excitement. I now knew a little more about Travis. These items belonged to him. As much as I wanted to leave the items, I knew I couldn't in case he returned and removed them—then our evidence would be lost forever.

I fetched a Ziplock bag I kept in the car in case I needed it. Before I did anything, I snapped a few photos of the grave, the hole, and the box then removed the contents with gloves and placed them inside the bag.

I closed the box and pushed the dirt back into the hole,

flattened it with my palms and placed the flowers where they belonged. I not only felt physically dirty but morally as well, like I'd tainted my soul by what I'd done. I'd stolen from the dead, like a graverobber, and an overwhelming sense of dread filled me. Although I felt terrible for taking the items, we had to know more about Travis. We needed to understand who exactly he was and where he came from—what he was really like. And, since he'd been so good at hiding his past, this was the only way I could find out.

Once I was on I-90 to Chicago, I headed straight for the office. It didn't make any sense returning to Seekster, as Aika would most likely be in her office. I would rather be at our office and show Marc what I'd found.

I saw Marc sitting with a client when I entered; the poor woman was crying over the photos in her shaking hands. I didn't envy her, even though her clothing was designer. She was well looked after with not a care in the world—well, that counted. If I remembered correctly, this one's husband had a string of women, one for every day of the week, and he kept Sundays for his wife. He was a very wealthy businessman, and her prenup would leave her with nothing if she divorced him. But that didn't mean she couldn't use the photos to mess with his career. I told Marc she needed to heed with caution, because men like that bowed down for no one. And, if he loved her so much that he still messed around on her, it would mean nothing for him to get rid of her if she threatened him. But it was her life, and she had information to do with as she pleased.

"Thank you, Marc," she whispered, tucked the photos into her handbag and wiped tears off her face. "And don't worry, I won't threaten him." She handed over the check. "This should cover everything."

Marc placed the check on his desk. "May I ask what you intend on doing with the photos?"

"I will be visiting his little whores. I'm pregnant, and I want my husband to understand where we stand, and I will make sure his *women* understand as well."

"Just be careful."

"I know the type of man he is. I know what I'm doing." She stood and left before Marc uttered another word.

"That went well," I said when I reached his desk. "Look what I found." I placed the bag of memorabilia on his desk.

"What's this?"

"It's Travis's—"

"How did you get these?" Marc asked with panic laced in his tone.

"Didn't you get my texts?"

"I've been busy." He reached for his cellphone from his drawer. Marc had instructed me to message him where and what I was doing for my safety, but it didn't help if his cellphone was in his desk. What if I had needed his help and he didn't hear the ringtone? Come to think of it, it was pointless sending him updates; he was busy and still had a business to run. "Did he see you?" Marc finally asked after reading my messages, sounding more relaxed than before.

"No, I doubt it. Like I said in my texts, it is his house Aika goes to every day. After she left, I followed his black car, and he stopped at a remote area near Woodstock. After he left, I went to see what was out there, and I found two gravestones where I assume he had buried his parents. And I found them"—I pointed at the photos—"in an old breadbox in the ground."

"He'd kill you for this alone."

"He's already after me. At least now I know a little more about the man."

"You're playing with fire, little one." Marc pulled on gloves and removed the contents. He held up the birth certificate. "But this is helpful."

"I want to keep this between us, and I certainly don't want to go digging. He might have a system in place to trace anyone who searches anything around his birth. Everything will have to be done in person." I placed my handbag in my desk drawer and plugged in my laptop and switched it on. I went to Marc's desk so we could browse the items together.

There were eight baby photos of a boy with dark hair. From the clothing they dressed him in and the quality of the photo, we assumed they were taken during the seventies and were Travis's baby pictures. He had been an adorable baby. His parents were good looking; his mom had dark brown almost black hair, long black eyelashes, with blue eyes, and silky skin. His dad was average to handsome, with blue eyes and thin lips; he wasn't ugly or drop-dead gorgeous but in-between—there was something about him I couldn't place my finger on. Both seemed as though they were tall. In one photo, they held baby Travis and stood in front of a window. Either the window was low or they were taller than average.

I picked up his birth certificate with gloved hands. He had been born on a leap year—February 29, 1980. That would make him thirty-five now and two years older than me. "Do you think we can find something at the hospital where he was born?"

"What information do you want to get from there? Back in the seventies, they hardly had as much paperwork to fill out as they do today. And there wasn't much in technology then either. We have his birth certificate with his name and date of birth. We could always ask Billie to find what he can. But, like you say, if he can trace when someone does a search on his family, I guarantee you he will do the same when someone does a search at the hospital where he was born. I would rather us try to follow him to find out what he's up to than do anything remote. At least he won't know we are digging. And we could use this as evidence when we go to the cops."

"Okay, that makes sense." As much as I hated to admit it, I couldn't go to the hospital. What was I hoping to gain? I had more of a chance by following him and getting his routine down than digging into his past. Perhaps that wasn't the only house he owned. If I followed him, I could see where else he frequented. Then when we had enough information, we could give it all to Donnie and James, and they could take it further. From what Johnny had said in previous conversations, after the altercation with Travis and his vigilante killers four years ago, there hadn't been any more body dumps with their similar MO. It was as if they had stopped doing what they did and vanished, but we knew it wasn't true. This was the perfect opportunity for me to know what he and the rest of them had done with the bodies. They had either moved their operation elsewhere or they had found an alternative way of disposing the bodies. Perhaps they had a warehouse filled with tanks of acid or near the ocean and dumped the bodies at sea.

My imagination ran away with me, and Marc said something, pulling me back into the present. "Sorry, what did you say?"

He chuckled. "I wanted to know if you've eaten. I'm about to order Chinese. I skipped lunch with my client being here. Perhaps we could grab an early dinner?"

"I'm meeting with Dr. Adams at four, but I can eat now, and you know what I want." I grinned.

Chapter Four

THE MEDICAL SUITES at Dr. Adam's office was quiet. The hallways were empty, and, for a moment, I thought I had the wrong date and time. I knocked on the door, and it opened slowly, as if the wind had blown it ajar. The receptionist had already left for the day, and his office door was wide open.

"Come in, Dana," he said.

His front office was cool, but, as I entered his office and closed the door, I felt the warmth.

"Come sit." He motioned for me to sit at the couch while he stood and walked around his desk, heading for his usual spot near the window.

"I thought I had mixed up the dates again."

"Oh, why do you say that?" He sat and crossed one leg over the other. He steepled his index fingers and concentrated on me. It was unnerving how he did that, like he wanted to know everything about me—inside and out. I supposed it was good to have a therapist who considered me that way, but it still shook me.

"Because it's so quiet here, and your receptionist has left for the day I thought everyone had left."

"We could always meet at an earlier time if you prefer?"

"Oh no, that's not what I'm saying. I was just confused."

"Do you get confused often?" His brows knitted together.

"No." My frown matched his. "That's not what I ... Never mind."

"What is it you are trying to say?" he asked sternly.

I exhaled a frustrated breath and tried again. "Just that the medical suites were quiet when I arrived. I expected more people. And before you say anything, I can't meet earlier than four o'clock. I need to work."

"Did you have a rough day?" He grabbed his notepad and ballpoint pen. He was about to write something but paused, waiting for me to speak.

Perhaps I was having another off day. The package we had received with Nigel's ashes may have gotten to me more than I thought. That our colleague and friend was a victim to Travis and his vigilante killers made me mad. And that it was possibly I may have found where Travis lived—well, I was sure it was his house. But, at the same time, doubt crept in about Aika, the others who were part of that group, and whether I could get any evidence on them and Travis. And now I may have gotten the dates and times of my appointments muddled when I hadn't really.

"I don't know." I sat back in the soft couch, kicked off my shoes and pulled my knees to my chest. "Maybe ... lots happened today."

"Do you want to talk about it?"

"I didn't want to say anything because I'm not sure, but I'm ninety-nine percent sure I've found where Travis lives." I couldn't help but smile.

"The man you think is out to kill you?" He arched an eyebrow.

"I don't *think* he is out to kill me, he *is* out to kill me. I've been following his colleague. You remember the one I spoke of last time—"

"Aika?" he read off his notepad.

"Yes, I've been following her for a few days, and she always goes to the same house around lunch time. At first, I thought it was strange or she was having an affair, because the house she goes to doesn't belong to her. Then, instead of following her back to the office, I went closer to the house, but I couldn't see anything. Then ...! He drove past me, and I decided to follow him!" I wasn't sure whether I should say anything more. I still felt guilty for taking the items from the breadbox.

"Did he see you following him?"

"No, I don't think so."

"How sure are you?" Dr. Adams cocked his head as he made his point.

And, as sure as I was while I was following Travis, I wasn't sure anymore. I bit my thumbnail. "Maybe? No, I am sure. If he saw me, he wouldn't have driven to his destination."

"Which was?"

"I really feel guilty about this, and I didn't want to tell you. I followed him and found unmarked gravestones I'm sure are his parents. And he buried something which I dug up."

"You're saying if he knew you were following him, he wouldn't have gone there?"

"No, he wouldn't have gone there. He would know I'd see his parent's grave and the items in the breadbox. It's photos of him as a baby and his birth certificate," I said quickly, hoping Dr. Adams wouldn't judge me for what I'd done.

"Did you remove the items?" he asked softly, not a whisper, but careful not to frighten me for confessing my sins.

I glanced at him. "I did, and I feel really terrible about it. But I want to know more about him. I want to understand where he came from and exactly what had happened to him."

"That turned him into the killer he is today?"

I nodded, still biting my thumbnail.

"Don't feel guilty, Dana. You were only doing what you thought was right. This man is an enigma, and you want to get to know him."

"Uh-huh. Exactly! There's hardly any information on him, and what we do know is sparse."

"Don't you think maybe he is trying to show you more of himself without scaring you? That perhaps he is opening up to you, little by little?"

I hadn't considered that, and blinked wide eyes at the doc.

"That perhaps he hasn't tried to contact you again because he doesn't mean you any harm—anymore? Perhaps he doesn't want to frighten you again."

A strange noise came from the back of my throat, almost a sarcastic laugh. I was as surprised by it as the doc was. "You're kidding, right? This man is dangerous and almost killed me … twice. If he were here right now, I'm sure he would slit my throat."

"Okay fine, I understand where you're coming from, but hear me out. What if he is trying to change? You said he helped you out on your last case, so maybe he is trying to make amends for what he's done in the past."

I really hadn't considered it that way. Maybe doc was on

the right path. "Maybe, I don't know. If he's trying to make amends, why kill Nigel?" I shrugged. "I don't know him well enough to make that statement or judgement. All I can speak to is what I've been through, and yes, this last case, he actually helped out—as creepy as that sounds. And he didn't come for me when I tried searching for him and his family even though he knows I've been looking into them." Then I remembered all those holes near Eugene's shallow grave. "That's probably what he dug up near Eugene's grave on Devil Mountain, the breadbox full of his stuff. He dug it up and buried it with his parents."

Dr. Adams continued with his speech on self-awareness and the homework I had to do every day. I informed him I hadn't had another panic attack, and even though we received Nigel's ashes, I didn't freak out—which was progress, and he agreed with me. He asked about James and how our relationship was going, which was still as perfect as could be. He was just very busy with a case he and Donnie were working on but said it should be finalized soon.

Our consultation went over time, and he didn't charge me for those fifteen minutes; he was just happy to see the progress I'd made and said I should only see him again in two weeks' time.

Chapter Five

TRAVIS

AIKA HAD LEFT a few moments ago, after our daily briefing. So far, she was making great strides in my company that I had enough confidence in her to continue with the daily engagements with the developers in my absence. It was a relief to know I'd finally found someone who could almost do the job as well as me. And, to top it off, I didn't feel like killing her—yet—even though we saw each other every day. I even enjoyed her company during lunch. I shouldn't get comfortable though. I'd been burned by people I trusted once too often. She was good at doing the things I'd asked her to do, but I understood where her true allegiance was, and it wasn't with me.

"I'm done for the day, Mr. Green," Cheryl said as she opened the kitchen door. Her handbag strap was over her shoulder, and with her other hand, she held the plate of food we had left over from lunch. At least she had dinner for her grandkids ready by the time she got home. I'd been letting her go home after lunch so she could spend more time with them after school. I didn't want her grandkids sitting in aftercare, wasting their precious lives doing homework and staring into four white walls while they waited for their only family member who cared for them. At least now Cheryl could take care of them and spend quality time and still get paid her full salary. Heaven knew she deserved more, and I made it my mission to care for them for the rest of their lives.

"Thanks, Cheryl," I said as I opened the door wider for her. "I will see you tomorrow."

"Yes, Mr. Green," she said and approached her car.

No matter how many times I'd told her not to call me by my formal name, she still did. She said she preferred to call me that while she worked under my roof; she didn't want to become complacent in her job. I couldn't agree more with her sentiments, but she was more than just an employee, she was my family after I'd lost my parents. She took care of me instead of shipping me off to lowlife relatives I didn't know about. I may only have been ten at the time when I had instructed my father's lawyers what I wanted, but they'd agreed with me. The estate sustained me financially and had paid Cheryl while she cared for me. She had been young and married with two kids of her own, but she had lived with me while her kids lived with her sister. Their deaths would be on my conscience for as long as I lived. If I hadn't been hogging their mother's attention, she would've been home for them and disciplining them. Cheryl's sister had been more relaxed and had allowed the boys to do what they wanted. As they got older, they became involved in gangs and ended up dead. I had made it my mission to ensure their children, Cheryl's grandkids, were well looked after and Cheryl was home for them after school.

I watched Cheryl leave, and the gate closed. I'd been so busy lately with Aika and assisting Dana with her case I'd neglected a few things, like a trip to my parents. But I had an ulterior motive.

Pulling out the driveway and easing down the street, I glanced to the side road and saw her car. The little sleuth had been following Aika to my house. I should have been upset she knew where I lived, but I wasn't. She was intelligent enough to pick up on a few things, and I suspected her conversation with Aika last week had sparked her interest. I'd already known this day would come, and Dana was smart enough to put the clues together. She had been the one who figured out my pattern all along. She had used the formation she had and knew where we would dump the bodies all those years ago. It would only be a matter of time before she discovered all the truth, before she discovered me. But she knew me more than she would admit to.

I allowed her to accompany me on my road trip. I wanted her to meet my parents. I wanted her to understand where I came from and who my parents were, what it truly meant to be a Green.

When I had the means and the knowledge, I had ghosted myself and that of my family to protect them and the little girl who would've shamed our family name. There were no grandparents or close living relatives who would have felt the shame, but there was my father's company and all his shareholders. If any of them had found out the little girl my mother had carried was not my father's, the company's share price would have fallen. The stock market's a fickle machine, the fluctuations either made or broke you, and this would've crushed the company as well as everything I owned.

Dana passed by when I turned onto the dirt road leading to my parents' final resting place. She was good at remaining unseen, but I knew she was there. I felt her gaze on me when I climbed out the car, the muted tones filled with an unheard lullaby of memories long forgotten. The beat of my heart filled my ears as the drumming vibrations surrounded me—the continuous sounds created by me, the rhythm of the day swirling around, and the rhythm inside of me. I felt her gaze on me again and smiled to myself as I walked toward the trees and crouched by their graves. Her being near was as wonderful as if she were right beside me, holding my hand. To know that she too would do what I was about to do exhilarated me. I buried the breadbox with a few pictures as well as my birth certificate so she could see who I really was. And I wanted her to come find me. I wanted her to come to *me*. And now that she knew where I lived would help me in the end. I knew where she was and didn't have to search for her when I was ready.

These four years, I'd kept her afraid and scared what I would do next. I reveled in her fear, but it made her soft. I'd made her tame. I'd made her weak. That's not the Dana I wanted. I wanted someone to stand up to me, to challenge me. To fight me. Now that she was ready, she could come after me.

After I'd left, I knew she would snoop to see what I was doing, and I was pretty sure she would remove the photos. I'd taken a left turn instead of getting back onto I-90 and drove up the hill to see what she was up to, and there she was, *my* Dana. She removed the items from the breadbox with a sad expression—her conscience eating at her. The last few months, I really got to know her, what made her tick, what made her upset, and how she was working through her nightmares. All I could say was I was very proud of her. She'd made great strides in not being so scared. The chase wouldn't have been so much fun if she were. As much as I liked to see them afraid, to piss their pants or cry, I didn't want to go after a little mouse. I wanted her to be my equal. I wanted her to fight as hard as she could and know when it was all over, she had done her best.

My apartment and compound had been ready for her arrival for quite some time already, and now that she was ready, I could show her what I had to offer.

Chapter Six

CALL it intuition or the fact that I may be crazy, but I returned to Seekster after my session with Dr. Adams and waited for Aika. The last few days I'd been following her, she always went home after work. As much as I'd rather go home right now and put up my feet, especially after the busy day I just had, but I wanted to ensure she went home and not somewhere else.

I spotted her car in the parking garage and waited. My legs were aching from sitting, but, if I climbed out my car and stretched, I would risk someone in that tall, ominous building seeing me. I switched on my laptop and browsed the emails I'd been ignoring all day and let James know where I was in case he came home early and I wasn't there.

It was around seven when she crossed the street. Her long raven hair was unmistakable in the sea of suits and dark dresses. She crossed the street with poise and grace, knowing full well businessmen gawked at her. She was stunning, but beneath all that exotic beauty was a woman who wouldn't think twice to cut off your head. If I had to guess which weapon was hers, I'd say knives. I imagined her holding delicate yet dangerous knives and cutting you into pieces.

She climbed into her red sports car and drove slowly from the garage then, once on the road, drove like a bat out of hell. Pulling from my parking spot without her seeing me and trying to stay with her proved tricky. The trip lasted twenty minutes, then she stopped at a building—a health and wellness center. I passed by, circled the block and came around again. Other vehicles were in the parking lot, and one of them belonged to Travis—his black Merc with the S for a numbered plate.

My curiosity was killing me. I needed to get inside.

If Aika and Travis were in the building, the possibility the others might be there as well was greater, and I could finally see who they were. But, for the life of me, I couldn't figure out why a health and wellness center.

I parked around the block and out of sight then walked toward the center. On the right was the service entrance I could use without detection. Wooden boxes stacked against the walls and the loading bay was clear with a door that stood wide open. I approached the door then slowly and carefully peered inside. The kitchen was empty. I crossed the kitchen floor and peered around the doorjamb into an empty corridor, but I heard voices.

I padded quietly across the hallway toward the voices and leaned against the wall near the doorjamb. The entrance to the center was to my right and a set of stairs to my left with doors on either side. Not wanting to risk being seen, I stayed there and listened to a few voices, each person speaking in turn. I caught some of the words but not all. It sounded like a support group for families who had lost a loved one. Someone was telling their story; his voice was gruff and filled with sadness. He'd lost a twin brother who had committed suicide. He rambled on about how much he missed his brother every day, and, with their parents gone, he was the only one left.

Another man spoke, another deep baritone. A drunk driver had killed his wife in a car accident and had managed to get off with only paying a fine. He had been charged with manslaughter, and his lawyer had found a way to get him off, all because he had the money and the means in which to do so. This man continued speaking, and, at first, I'd mistaken him for crying until he burst into laughter, then I heard clearly, "I know! The best part was when he rolled out of the tarp and into the middle of the road," the man said, followed by more laughter. "He looked like a dead fish."

"Yeah, then those agents showed up and ruined our fun," another man said, and everyone laughed again. "Gosh, has it been four years already? It feels like just the other day we started."

I gasped and pressed my hands firmly against my mouth. It was them. All of them. My eyes stung. The back of my throat burned. My clothing clung to my body. I tried to steady my breathing. I wanted to hyperventilate. My chest ached. If they heard me, that would be it. I was outnumbered, and they would hurt me. They would kill me.

I needed to calm down. I exhaled slowly. Wiped my eyes dry. After a moment, I relaxed, and the stars were no longer clouding my vision. It dawned on me this was how they had met. This was it. They met at this support group. It made perfect sense. They had each lost a loved one and had their revenge, and they had helped each other kill so nobody could tell on each other.

"Yeah, and that stupid cow arrived—"

29

"You've been warned before, Dafne. Don't make me angry," *he* said.

And I knew who he was. It was *him*. My arms pebbled. I was so close, so dangerously close, but I couldn't do anything. Not yet, not now, not like *this*. If I burst through the doors with only my weapon and the six of them drew theirs, I would be dead in seconds. That would be the end of everything. I had to plan this carefully. I needed to figure out who each of them was, what they did, where they came from and, of course, what they looked like—I couldn't stick my head around the corner and say *hi*. Currently I only knew what Aika looked like, and now this—their rendezvous point. I still needed to figure out how often they came here; was it only Wednesday evenings, or was it more often?

I was so excited and happy and wanted to phone Marc to tell him my discovery but not yet, I had to get out first. Slowly, one step at a time, I crossed the hallway toward the kitchen area. Their voices grew louder as their meeting ended.

"We should go to your bar, Travis, or are you still having it repainted?"

A bar? Travis owned a bar somewhere. I needed to follow them and find out where this bar was. As I reached the kitchen, the door slammed, followed by footsteps heading for me. I couldn't turn around and go back or I would walk straight into them. Their voices grew louder as they approached the hallway. I was trapped. The footsteps in the kitchen neared. I didn't have anywhere else to go but toward the end of the hallway and near the stairs. Not knowing where they were heading, I strode to the end of the hallway. As quickly and quietly as I could, I walked along the shadows of the corridor, trying the doors along the way for one that opened. The footsteps grew louder as the person came through the kitchen and into the passage. The voices from the office were louder than before as they joked about something I wasn't privy to. The person from the kitchen entered the hallway as I slipped into the bathroom.

My pulse hammered in my ears as I leaned against the closed door. There was no way I could go back out there. I needed to find a way out. I went into the last stall and locked it. I closed the toilet lid and climbed onto it. As I reached for the window, the bathroom door opened. I quickly sat on my haunches and held my breath. Footsteps neared as the person entered, water splashed in the sink, and the door opened and closed again. I exhaled a shaky breath, stood upright on the toilet seat and peered over the top—the door was closed, and the bathroom was empty. Behind me, the window was ajar. With one hand, I pushed open the window and lifted myself up and over. I climbed out slowly as the bathroom door opened again. I fell out the window, still gripping the frame; one foot dangled in the air while the other still hooked on the windowsill. Luckily, the last window could not be seen from the door, and they couldn't see me, but they could hear me if I moved too quickly.

"Someone is here, I'm telling you," a man said.

"Who?" a woman asked.

My groin pulled as I did the splits. As quietly as possible, I lifted my boot off the windowsill and dropped to the ground, crouched as I regained my balance and ran to the end of the building. I didn't want to stay to find out who that was. Peering around the corner, I ensured nobody was in the alley near the loading zone. I sprinted to the end, and again, I looked before I pushed on. Their cars were still there, but nobody was around. They were still inside. I ran to my car, climbed inside and burst into tears. That was too close—way too close.

When I was calm, I started the engine. I wanted to follow one of the others to profile them, then at least I would know three of them. I slowly approached the center, and their cars were gone.

"No!" I slammed my hand on the steering wheel. They had just been here a moment ago, and I'd missed them somehow. They must've hightailed it out of there when that person followed me into the bathroom. I drove as fast as I could to the end of the street, looking left and right, but it was empty; there was no red sports car and no black Merc. I could not have taken longer than two minutes to recover when I had climbed into my car.

Unless it had taken me longer without realizing it ...

Chapter Seven

I TOOK A LEFT, as if driving back to Seekster. I wasn't sure where they had gone, but I wasn't about to stop trying. They could've gone the other way and be long gone, but I knew what Aika's car looked like, and I knew Travis's car; surely, I could spot one of them if they went this way. A red car caught my attention, and I headed in that direction. As I neared, I recognized her car with the black Merc ahead of her with four other cars behind hers. As I reached the tail end of the line of cars, I slowed down.

They took a left onto Michigan Avenue, drove past stores and buildings then stopped outside a house. I drove past and turned right at the streetlight to circle back, using a quiet road without buildings to block my view, only a playground with a school on the opposite side. They parked all six cars on the property. Lights were on inside the house. I parked, climbed out and approached with caution. With an app on my phone, I sent Marc my location.

He replied quickly with a red-faced and swearing emoji. *Do not approach. It's dangerous, only watch.*

I'm not going inside, promise, I replied then pocketed the cellphone.

The three-story house they had entered stood on its own with a flat roof reminiscent of a castle wall. To the right of it were two houses that shared the same wall between them. To the left of their house was an open lot with neatly cut grass. If I had to guess, I would surmise this was an old neighborhood, and there had been more houses here, but, as time went on, houses got knocked down with only a few remaining. This had to be the bar they had mentioned at the center.

I crouched low and ran under the window toward the back door. As I turned the corner, the red light above a camera caught my eye, and I backpedaled, hoping I wasn't seen. I noticed no cameras were on this side of the house. I couldn't risk being recorded, so I stayed where I was under the window. On tiptoes, I peered inside to see six people sitting around a bar on the right side. Aika sat at the back, and all I saw were heads of hair, not faces.

My cellphone vibrated in my pocket. I saw it was James asking me where I was.

Laughter erupted inside. Someone poured drinks, and they spoke loudly. A man with black hair stood and put his arm around another man with his back to me. They laughed. A woman with white hair sipped on a glass of wine. A man with copper-colored hair joined the one with black hair and placed his arm around the shoulders of the guy who had his back to me. Another man with a shaved head stood behind the bar, pouring drinks for everyone.

Travis wasn't bald, and he didn't have copper-colored hair. He was either the one with black hair or had his back to me. The woman with the white hair raised her glass and said a toast. "This is for your lady. May you find her and finally make her yours." The man with his back to me nodded, raised his glass of whiskey and downed it. The guy with the black hair went behind the bar. I could see his face now, and he was a little older—perhaps in his forties. He wasn't Travis, who was in his mid-thirties. Travis had to be the one with his back to me.

It was cold outside. It was only October, and a chill hung in the air. I hugged my jacket around my body, and my legs ached. The area was quiet with minimal passing cars, and the neighbors to my left were indoors and most likely watching TV, if the sounds I heard were correct.

A glass broke inside, and I peered through the window again. After more laughter, they stood and set down their empty glasses. Travis still had his back to me as he brought up the rear and switched off the light. Their laughter filled the quiet night as they exited the house, and I fell flat on my stomach. I crawled to the corner to see the front of the house. Sharp blades of grass poked at my fingers while stones dug into my hips and sides. This was not fun. Luckily, this side of the house had no lights, and I was bathed in darkness.

They climbed into their respective cars and left.

I wanted to follow one of the others so I knew at least three of them, but I couldn't risk running to my car now or they would see me. The last to exit the house with the bar was Travis. Again, I couldn't see his face. The streetlamp didn't work and had cast his face in shadows. Aika left in her red Mustang after the woman with white hair. Travis climbed into his black car and left. I was still on the ground, trying to stay hidden. When I was positive he was gone, I groaned, climbing to my feet. My knees, stomach, and hips ached from lying on the ground. I dusted grass from the front of my body and crossed the street to my car.

Travis

Once Neal had poured everyone a drink, I had to ask the burning question. "Okay, who was it?" I glared at each of my Horsemen. "Who was at our center tonight?"

Everybody stared at each other, but no one said anything.

"Dammit, you better not be lying to me." I white-knuckled the bottle in my hand.

Aika wrapped her arm around me and squeezed gently. "We don't know, Travis. I swear."

All their heads bobbed up and down.

"It could've been a stranger needing the bathroom."

"Don't patronize me, Aika," I removed her hand from my shoulder. "The person escaped through the bathroom window. If it was a stranger needing the bathroom, they would've left the same way they entered."

"Malcom probably scared them off, Travis. He isn't exactly the calmest person around." Aika giggled. "Why worry about it?"

I grabbed her hand and squeezed it, slightly twisting her wrist.

She flinched and moved, trying to ease the pain in her arm. "Ease up, Travis, you're hurting me."

I released her hand and pushed her away from me. "Now is not the time to mess around. We need to be careful what we do and what we say. Eyes and ears are everywhere."

"You're being paranoid, Travis," Damian said, consoling Aika. "As far as we know, you're the only one watching our every move. We know you're spying on us, even when we aren't together."

I pursed my lips and exhaled through my nose. I needed

to remain calm. "I just need everyone to be more careful than usual."

"For all we know, you're the one bringing others to us. What about that girl? Dana? You've been bent on her for the last four years." Neal stepped backward and raised his hands. "I'm just saying, Travis, stop looking at us. We know what would happen if we did anything wrong, and neither of us wants to go to jail. I suggest we get rid of that woman once and for all—"

"That's enough!"

Everybody flinched.

"No one is going after her. She isn't your concern, and I keep tabs on her."

"Everybody calm down," Joe interjected, always trying to keep the peace between us. "Neal, we leave Dana alone. And, Travis ..."

I glanced up and leered at him.

"We are not your enemy, brother. We are in this together. Remember that." He placed a calm hand on my shoulder. "Now, Neal, please give us all shooters. I think we need to relax and have a couple of laughs."

After the shot of whiskey, I calmed down. But that didn't mean I liked it. No way my Dana had entered the center. No way. She wouldn't do that. I needed to follow my Horsemen to ensure none of them were doing anything behind my back. It had to be them.

Dafne kept glancing in my direction, waiting for me to lose my shit again, but I wouldn't entertain her. And Aika offered me her pathetic sympathetic expression.

I plastered on a smile and continued joking with them. I would need to review a few videos.

Chapter Eight

JAMES PACED in front of me while I sat on the couch with my hands in my lap. "What were you thinking?" he asked for the second time.

I'd shrugged the first time he asked instead of answering. "I wasn't thinking—"

"No, you weren't. You cannot go around doing that, *Dana*." He punctuated my name to emphasize his anger over me following the vigilante killers. "What if they saw you? Promise me you won't do this again." He towered above me as shadows played on his face, his very angry face. He'd never been this angry before and certainly not at me.

"I promise," I whispered.

"I'm serious. Not again." He sat beside me, pulled me into the curve of his body and kissed the top of my head. "You must be careful."

We sat like that for a few minutes, and it felt good, comforting.

"Are you hungry?"

"Not really," I said.

While James ate, I told him about the rest of my day, and his hard expression softened, and he relaxed—even laughed. I understood where his anger came from, but it was an opportunity I couldn't pass up. If I'd called him first and waited for either him or Donnie to arrive and continue what I'd started, we might have lost them. If I didn't go into the center, I wouldn't have known it was their group session and that it was *them*—all six of the vigilante killers in one place. And then I wouldn't have known to follow them to the bar, which also belonged to Travis.

Billie had searched Travis, even on the dark web, and had found nothing. Travis had most likely used corporations to buy property he used personally, hence they were all untraceable under his name. Without any other information to go on, we were stuck, so me discovering the other properties was like striking gold.

For the first time since they started their killing spree four years ago, I now knew who they were, almost. I saw their faces, and now I had two places where they frequented, which James and Donnie could investigate further, along with Billie. It was a start, a freakin' great start as well.

After dinner, we sat on the couch and watched reruns. When I fell asleep on James's shoulder, he ushered me to bed.

Chapter Nine

THURSDAY

I PRESSED THE INTERCOM, and Billie's voice boomed, "What? Oh, it's you. Come on through."

The large iron gates slowly opened. I drove through and watched in the rearview mirror as they closed behind me.

Billie waited in the doorjamb, holding a bottle of water. "To what do I owe the pleasure this fine morning? Next time, call ahead. I could have visitors."

"You never have visitors, Billie. We are all you've got."

He chortled and waved the bottle in my face. "That's what you think. Come on, then tell Uncle Billie everything you need."

I sat in one of his La-Z-Boy chairs while Billie tapped on his keyboard. I gave him Travis's birth certificate and asked if he could find anything now that we had his birth-date. Previously we didn't have that information, only names. "Do the ME's office make copies of death reports?"

"They should. Why?"

"You couldn't get any of that info when you first investigated his parents' death, and the police report was missing chunks of information, and none of it was captured in the system due to the data leak—"

"Their system crashed," he corrected.

"Right." I sat upright in the chair. "I want to see if there's anything worth hiding."

"What could they be hiding?"

"That's what I want to find out. Why would Travis want to hide his family? I could understand he wanted to hide himself, his name, where he came from, from everyone, but why his parents and their death?"

Billie exhaled audibly. "They might only have physical copies at the ME's office. Not sure if you want to go back to Devil Mountain though."

"No, I don't. I don't want Travis to know what I'm doing."

"And you think he won't know we're snooping into his parents' death? He's smart, Dana. Don't forget that."

"I haven't forgotten." I sounded irritated to myself and knew Billie picked up on my tone. Now that I thought about it, I needed Billie to check who owned the house where the vigilante killers enjoyed a drink or two and if any names were associated with the support group session from last night.

"You could've phoned and asked me to do all this. You didn't have to come here in person. Why aren't you at work anyway?"

"Marc knows I'm here. You don't have to tattletale on me. And I don't want to discuss this over the phone, and, if you have anything for me, I would rather be here. I'm just being careful, that's all."

Billie peered at me over the rims of his glasses then pushed them up his nose. "Fine, get comfortable, this may take all day. If you don't mind, you might have to call the ME's office if I can't get anything online."

"Fine by me." I opened my laptop to check my work emails. I had no client appointments for the rest of the week; therefore, I could work anywhere, and Marc was happy with that. He wanted me to relax a bit, and this was a way for me to do just that.

My neck ached due to the position I was working in and was relieved when Billie finally came up for air. He'd been typing on his computers for two hours when he eventually pushed back his chair, folded his arms across his soft belly and gave me a satisfactory smile.

"You found something?"

"I found a few somethings." He emphasized the *s*.

I quietly hoped he had found juicy pieces of somethings.

He grinned as he spoke. "Now, it was hard, I might add, but it was rewarding once I knew what I was looking for."

"I hate it when you do this. Can you just tell me, already?"

The printer made a screeching sound as it spat out its paper. Billie reached for it and read the page before handing it over. "This could be the reason why Travis hid their deaths. What I'm about to give you may be his driving force."

"Tell me, already!" I sat on the edge of my seat.

"At the ME's office, they captured the DNA samples of his mom and dad. They discovered a third."

"What?" I stood, reaching for the paper.

"It had similarities with the mom, though, but not the dad."

"Really?" I asked, as Billie handed it to me. I read the information and felt my jaw slacken. "A baby? There was a baby girl, and she too died that day."

Billie nodded.

"And Travis's father wasn't the dad."

"Correct!" He pushed his chair toward the printer and again it made that ear-piercing sound as it spat out more paper. "At first, I thought it was only because he had killed his parents, that there couldn't possibly be any other reason why Travis killed Eugene, but, when I saw that"—he pointed to the paper in my hand—"I knew that had to be the connection. I've been doing this job for too long not to be able to connect these dots. And well, luckily, I'd found Eugene's DNA based on the latest results the ME captured when you found his remains. He had similarities with the little girl."

"No way!" I grabbed the other paper from Billie's hands to read it for myself. It matched up. It all made sense now. "As much as I hate this guy for what he's done, I can understand why he did it though. It was his parents, his unborn sister, and he was only ten years old when he witnessed their murder, and he couldn't do anything to protect them. Then, as he got older—and wiser, I think—he killed the man who took them away from him. If I think about what he'd done with his vigilante killers, they too couldn't protect their loved ones. Then when someone took them away, they became the protectors and killed the bad guy. As much as I hate to admit this, I get why they did what they did. I really do." I sat back in the comfortable chair. "I think if someone had hurt one of my parents, Donnie, or his family and even James, I might do the same."

"I totally get it, Dana, but I lost my parents when I was young too. They were killed, murdered in this house while I was sleeping a few rooms away. Someone broke into our house and slaughtered them like animals. The only reason I lived was because they couldn't find me. This house is so big that by the time they were looking for me, the cops were on their way because of the alarms. I hid in the closet until a policewoman pulled me out." Red flecks blossomed Billie's chubby cheeks. "You don't see me killing anyone. You don't see me grabbing people off the street because they bumped into someone on the subway. The law is there for a reason, and we cannot take it into our own hands." Billie never got angry, but he was angry over what I'd said.

"I'm sorry. I didn't mean to upset you. And I completely agree. What he did, what they did, is wrong. The only thing I meant by it was I understand Travis a little better now."

"It's not you who upset me. It's this whole situation. Don't you ever wish you could just get out? Stop everything and get off this fast train before it derailed?" He stood and paced. He bunched his hands into fists then stopped pacing —I'd never seen Billie like this before. Whatever I'd said must've been a trigger for him. "I mean, I get it, but everybody has shit in their lives they can't just wipe away with murder and someone else's blood on their hands. And it never solved anyone's sadness by killing another person. Taking a life for a life. That circle of never-ending murder just keeps hurting. What would you do if I was out there, doing what they did? Would you agree with the sentiment you just made, or would you want me behind bars? What if I went after your dad because he gave the wrong financial advice and that person's company failed? It never stops, Dana. Do you understand?" His voice raised. "It will never end until we put a stop to it. To stop them." By the end of his speech, he was yelling.

I swallowed the lump in my throat, and my eyes pricked. When I could trust my voice and didn't feel so intimidated by Billie's glare, I finally responded. "Are you okay?"

"No!" he belted out and left the room. "You should go!"

"What about the other stuff?" I yelled back at him. When he didn't answer, I approached his printer and saw another page containing the corporation name that held the lease of the house Travis and his vigilante killers used as a bar. But there was no mention of a support group Wednesday evenings at the health center. Again, there were no other names or addresses, just more information that sent me in circles. But at least now we had another motive for why Travis had killed Eugene: to avenge his baby sister.

"Thanks, Billie!" I yelled into his house from the foyer. "I'm sorry if I upset you," I said as I closed the front door.

I had no idea where all that came from, and I didn't want to push any more of his buttons. He felt strongly about revenge, and I would respect his wishes, and I would never, ever mention it again. I didn't like angry Billie. Perhaps we shouldn't use him for a while. Give him some space. I wanted to yell that he should take a vacation but didn't want to put my foot in my mouth any more than I already had. I closed the door and left.

Chapter Ten

THE FIRST THING I did was call Marc about Billie's discovery regarding Travis's sister, and he told me to work the rest of the afternoon from home. He was out of the office and didn't want me there alone while he worked a case. He would feel better and knew James would agree if I was at home with the alarm on.

I had already read all my work emails and had no new cases to tend to, so I flipped through the television channels and found nothing interesting enough to watch, and I hated sports. James and Donnie were working a case, so James would be home later. I would be home alone for at least another eight hours. I was instructed to activate the alarms. James had installed two different alarms from two different security companies—one for the outer perimeter and one for the interior. I was safe if I stayed inside and didn't open for anyone. I felt claustrophobic inside my own home, but it was what I had to endure to stay safe, especially if I was home alone.

Since I no longer worked weekends—Marc's orders—I

thought of the plans James and I had made for the weekend. I had taken off tomorrow so we could leave early in the morning and spend the weekend at a cabin near a lake, but our plans had been cancelled because James was busy with this case. From the sounds of it, this case was taking up a lot of their time but also might be closing soon; I could only hope. When I had cancelled our reservation and had told Marc, he had said I still had to take off tomorrow, hence the reason for my boredom and the anxiety of being alone and doing nothing.

I wasn't allowed to work weekends, because no case was so urgent we had to work during our off days. Marc had said if the case was urgent, the client had to go to the cops. Now I didn't know what I would do with myself, and an uneasy feeling settled in the pit of my stomach. This was my first weekend home to do as I pleased, but I would also be alone. I wasn't one for shopping or pampering, while sitting and watching television didn't seem like time well spent either. If James was with me, we could have gone away like we had planned, perhaps hike, swim in the cold water, then sit by the fire with a glass of wine. And since I would be alone, I had to either stay locked up at home or go to the mall with my mother. I loved her dearly, but I didn't enjoy shopping with her; she read every single tag on each piece of clothing and stopped at every shop. It was torture for me.

Checking the clock, I harrumphed that only two minutes had passed. I watched Blaire Thorne kill a vampire on a new television show, and only a minute had passed. I switched off the screen and threw the remote onto the table, but it bounced off and landed on the floor. Sighing, I stood, picked it up and placed it on the table.

It was only two in the afternoon. I'd spent a good chunk of my morning with Billie, and since I'd missed tailing Aika to her lunch date with Travis, I couldn't do much while she was at work. I could always go straight to Travis's house and see if he was up to anything, perhaps take a peek inside his yard again, or I could follow him around.

Before I could argue with myself, I climbed into my vehicle and went for a drive. I first drove past his gate and saw his black Merc parked in front of the open garage door. Either he was on his way out or he'd just come back; I still wanted to get a closer look. After circling the block, I parked near Travis's home on the side again, like I had previously. I walked the back end of his block and entered the same house I had yesterday. The side gate was still open and the house still empty. I walked alongside the fence that bordered the two houses, and I heard someone speaking outside and most likely pacing from the way his voice muffled then grew louder as he walked away and back again, but I couldn't decipher any of his words. Then the sliding door closed. I wanted to get a better look.

Once I was on the house's porch, I could see into Travis's property. His pool had its cover on, and his glass house was shut tight—but I'd just heard him, so he must be home somewhere and most likely in one of the rooms.

As I turned around, I walked straight into someone's chest.

———

I AWOKE ON MY STOMACH, and my vision was blurry. No matter how quickly I blinked, I couldn't see much of anything. I wiped drool from my face and tried to sit upright. My thoughts were cloudy, and my body felt like lead.

Groaning, I managed to flip onto my back with a heavy

oomph from the effort. One thing for certain, I was on a comfortable bed. I stared at the ceiling and at my reflection in the very large mirror, and immediately it left a bad taste in my mouth. At least I could use the mirror to see more of the room as my body slowly revived. I saw a couch to my right and an open door to my left that looked like it could be the bathroom. Slowly, leaning on one elbow at a time, I moved so slow it felt like a metal helmet was on my head. I saw a door ahead of me. My arms and legs tingled, and I shook them, hoping to rekindle circulation. I slowly sat upright and scooted off the bed; my shoes touched the floor, and I stretched my legs. Two doors were to my left—one a closet and the other a bathroom. Scanning the tiny bachelor room, I saw a note on the bedside table. I crawled across the bed to grab it.

Hey sleepyhead,
   Welcome to your new home ...
   I'll see you around seven.
   Be ready for my arrival.
   T

My chest heaved as I sucked in air. Reading that note was like a shot of adrenaline to get my body to work; fight or flight instincts kicked in, and I wanted to run away. Trying not to hyperventilate, I ran to the bathroom and splashed water on my face, which tingled from the chloroform he had used on me. After I wiped my face dry, I glanced around. On the side of the bath sat a neatly folded bath towel with a facecloth on top of it—both starched white. The medicine cabinet held a new bar of soap, toothbrush, toothpaste, and roll-on deodorant. A miniature perfume bottle in the shape of a leaf smelled very florally, and, as much as I hated to admit it, it smelled wonderful. There was no shower, only a toilet, sink, and bath.

I knew he had locked me inside an apartment or a room, but I tried the front door anyway, even though I knew it would be locked. I noticed a panel on the side which used a keycard to open the door. The door had a peephole but no handle on the inside of the room, therefore no way for me to pick the lock. This was most probably the only apartment here, on top of some building in the middle of where exactly, I had no idea. I needed to get to grips with my predicament and understand the type of room I was in and if there was a way out.

The closet had four outfits neatly folded on one shelf with three pairs of underwear. I shuddered to think he had selected them for me; they were lace and expensive. And, he would most likely want something from me in return. I pushed the thoughts away and focused on the bedroom come living room which reminded me of a bachelor pad but for the poor kidnapped girl locked in a tower.

I inventoried the room again, slowly this time—a strange mirror on the ceiling, crisp white walls, a bathroom door, and a handle-less front door. There were no other windows except for a row of small windows that stretched from one end to the next where the two roofs joined at an odd angle and brought in some natural sunlight. The bathroom had no window; it was just a curtain against a wall with an extractor fan. The closet was just that. The bedside table held an alarm clock and the display read, 4:35 p.m. I had two and a half hours to get out of here.

Rubbing my hands after hitting the door, I paced— twenty-five wide steps from one side of the room to the front door. If I stayed here longer than an hour, it would drive me nuts. I felt like a caged animal. I could never stay here, live here for the rest of my life or until he got bored with me and decided to end my life. I would rather claw my way out of here then to be his whatever slave this was. I would at least know what he looked like, but how would I escape? He would overpower me again or drug me, then what? As I paced, I chewed on my bottom lip. Travis would most likely end up killing me if I stayed here. No, I had to find a way to get out now.

I glanced up at the windows; that was my only way out of here.

I placed the bedside table on the edge of the bed, hoping I could at least reach the windows. I steadied myself against the wall and stretched toward the window. I could touch it but not grab the handle to open the window. I had to get closer.

Once I was off the bed, I tried to push it toward the windows, but it didn't budge. I lifted the covers and saw it was bolted to the floor. Each leg contained a chain and shackles with padding inside so whoever wore them wouldn't get hurt. My arms pebbled at the thought. Determination washed over me, and a surge of adrenaline coursed through my veins.

I searched the bedside tables for anything I could use to open the window, and all I found was a couple of books, nail polish, and a nailfile. I grabbed the nailfile and climbed my tower again. I balanced with one foot on the bedside table, one foot against the headboard, a hand on the windowsill and the other trying to open the window. Holding my breath to steady my hand movements, the nailfile reached the window, and I leaned closer. My arms strained as I pressed the nailfile against the handle and watched it move. My hand shook as I pushed it farther, and the window clicked open. I exhaled a shaky breath and blinked rapidly; I didn't have a free hand to wipe tears just yet. Gripping the nailfile, I pushed open the window and was grateful it didn't swing shut but stayed in place.

My arms burned, and my thighs shook as I stood still, maintaining my balance. If I climbed off the bed, I was afraid I would be too exhausted to try again—or worse, if I didn't do something now, I could fall and hurt myself. It wasn't that far to the floor, but I could still get hurt. The window was open, and now was my one and only chance.

Pocketing the nailfile, I now could use both hands as I leaned against the wall near the window. I had to jump and grab the windowsill then pull myself out. I counted backward from three; it was now or fall and break a leg. "Three, two, one ..." I kicked, pushing myself away from the headboard and up. The bedside table flew off the bed as I gripped the windowsill with both hands.

"Argh!" I screamed as I hoisted myself. My arms wobbled, and with everything I had left, I pushed myself through the window. Lying on my elbows and belly, I caught my breath. I was halfway there; my legs dangled inside the room while my upper body was outside. If I dared to relax, I would fall out the window and crash to the floor.

The air outside was wonderful as I tasted freedom. I sucked in fresh air and exhaled another shaky breath, wiping away a rogue tear. Now all I had to do was get the rest of my body out. I swung my left leg up and onto the windowsill and pushed my body until I was completely on the roof. I could not see the ground below; the roof was at least flat, so I didn't slide to my death. Exhaling sharply, my body trembled after the arduous exercise, and I sat on the roof until my sea legs steadied and I could move with little shaking.

I no longer had my cellphone or a watch, so I had no

idea of the time, but the effort from climbing up here had taken at least forty minutes. That would make it after 5 p.m. I still had about two hours to get out of here. On hands and knees, I crawled to the edge of the roof and slowly peered over. I was at least ten floors up. I couldn't scale down the walls like Spiderman. I crawled around on top of the small roof and couldn't find a fire escape, ladder, rope or anything. Feeling a deep sense of frustration, and the urge to give up even though I knew I couldn't afford to. This couldn't be the end of it and there was no way I would climb back inside that tiny room. I needed a break and five minutes would help to collect my thoughts and build my energy reserves. I lay down and stared at the sky. I spotted another roof behind me. I was so consumed with looking below I didn't bother looking up. Sitting quickly, I crawled to where the wall of another building touched the one I was on. I saw a ladder, and I could only hope that building had a fire escape.

I climbed the ladder, my arms and legs trembling from the effort, but adrenaline was my friend today, and I found myself on another roof with an opened door—an exit. Tears streaked my face as I ran down the stairs, wiping my eyes with the back of my hand.

Chapter Eleven

I SAW no residents as I descended the stairs. The building was eerily quiet, as if still waiting for tenants to move in. Once I reached the ground floor and exited, I needed to discern where I was. I glanced left and right at both buildings, and neither had a name. Scanning the twelve floors, I ascertained the building on the left had the apartment where I had been held, with a black glass entrance door. A plaque hung on the wall inside, but I didn't want to risk going in, in case I couldn't get out again. The building on the right, the one I'd escaped from, was empty with a *For Sale* sign plastered on the wall. No wonder nobody else was in the building at the same time. Strange it was open—anyone could walk in and squat. I didn't care, just relieved I had escaped with minimal problems.

I strode to the end of the block. With each step, I felt pain in my hips and arms from climbing out the window. It felt as though I had scraped my body raw over rocks. When I saw a cab, I waved it down and asked him to take me home. The cab driver drove at a leisurely pace which helped me calm down. I'd caught my breath; my heart was no longer in my throat, and I could swallow. It was a relief to escape that apartment. I didn't want to imagine what he would've done to me if I'd stayed. And what was worse, it looked like it had been used before me.

Pushing violent thoughts aside, I noticed the cab was already in my neighborhood. I teared up when he parked outside my house. I told him to wait while I fetched cash from my safe and paid him. Once back inside my house, I locked the doors, activated the alarms and, using my home phone, called James.

"Hey, babe," he said, and I could hear the smile behind his soothing words.

I wanted to speak to him so badly, but I didn't want to break down. But, when he answered and sounded so good, I burst into a fit of tears.

"What's the matter? Did something happen?"

I made strange choking sounds from sobbing uncontrollably.

"Hey, Donnie! Can we go to your sister quickly? I think something's happened," he shouted at Donnie. "I'm coming, babe. Are you at home? And are you alone?"

"Uh-huh, I'm at my house. It was closer," I managed to spit out. "Please don't hang up. I need to hear your voice until I see you."

James stayed on the line with me until they arrived. James and Donnie almost broke my front door trying to get in. By then, I'd made myself some tea and had calmed down. After I made them coffee, I explained what had happened. Donnie's expression made me fearful, while James's was a combination of anger that I'd allowed myself to get kidnapped and happiness that I was still alive.

"Why do you always do this, Dana?" James scolded me

like a child. "You know what this guy is capable of doing, but you keep doing stupid things that put your life in danger. When are you ever going to learn?"

"Hey, that's enough," Donnie said, sticking up for me. He came to me and draped his arm around my shoulders. "She's been through enough without you yelling at her." He squeezed my shoulder and let go, but I still clung to him.

"I know, Donnie, but she doesn't listen—"

"I'm sorry!" I yelled. "I'm sorry. I thought I would be okay. I didn't know he was watching me."

"He is always watching you, Dana. If there's one thing you need to know, it's that. This guy is always watching you. For some reason, he's left you alone for four months, but not anymore. Next time, you aren't coming back." James folded his arms and exhaled.

I let go of Donnie to go to James who, at first, didn't move; he just stared down at me. Finally, he opened his arms and squeezed the life out of me. I buried my face into his chest and breathed him in. His embrace was comforting and I didn't want to let go.

"I know a private firm who can protect her at short notice while we're working. Our resources are scarce at the moment and doubt captain could spare any," James said after a moment's silence. "You need to give us everything you have on him so we can move this up the chain of command. Maybe get the FBI involved."

"I can help cover the cost."

"I've got it covered." James released me and pulled his cellphone out his pocket. "I'm just going to make the call quick," he said and exited the house.

"Are you okay?" Donnie arched an eyebrow.

"I'm fine. I escaped before he could do any of that." I said and sat at the kitchen counter.

"James is right you know. You need to stop going off on your own like that. And what made it worse, you didn't tell anyone—"

"I know. I said I was sorry."

"Dana, I know you are tough and can handle yourself, but this guy is something completely off the charts. He is dangerous and should not be approached."

I nodded, biting my lip.

"We will handle it from now on. Marc says you went to Billie today. What did you find?"

I handed over the documents along with any other piece of information we'd found and explained it all.

Donnie folded the pages and stuck it into his back pocket. "It'll be hard to convince a judge, but I will chat to Captain Dodd about this and have Travis followed. If we can spare two cops on surveillance, it could make you safe as well. We need to do more until we have enough evidence to build a case, okay?"

"Okay, it's all yours now. I won't do anything more, and I won't follow Aika anymore either—"

"For your safety, it's better if you don't."

"I said I won't, and I won't. I will just do my case load and that's it."

"Good."

"Okay, a man named Wayne will be arriving soon. He will be your shadow. He will stay where you stay. When you come to me, I will set up the spare bedroom for him. If you are here, he stays here," James said, walked into the kitchen and grabbed an apple from the fridge. "When he gets here, we have to head out again."

"Are you serious? You guys are still working?"

"Yeah," Donnie said, eyeing James. "This is another case I can't wait to be done with."

Chapter Twelve

THE TALL BUILDING of a man stood like a thunderous cloud on steroids. Wayne was tall, dark, and scary. His clothing was tight around his upper body and I thought his clothing might shred when he walked. His voice was deep, and I felt his words vibrate in my bones, shaking me to the core. I would not want to be on the receiving end on whatever he dished out; it would either maim or kill you. Seeing him was a shock to my system, if only I'd stayed at home and watched tv I wouldn't have gotten into trouble. But here we were and I had to suffer the consequences.

Wayne did a sweep of my house after Donnie and James had left, while I followed him around like a lost puppy.

"You don't have to watch me do this you know," Wayne said stopping dead in his tracks. He stared down at me like I was an ant he would love to squish.

"I know," I said, giving him one of my sweet smiles. "I've never had someone like you come in here to," —I gestured for him to continue, — "and I would like to learn."

"Fine, just stay out of my way."

Wayne sounded cranky so I didn't want to stand too close to him in case he swatted me away like a fly. I stayed in the passage while he checked all the bedrooms. When he was content that Travis was not here and no way for him to gain entrance into my house, he entered the living room and peered behind the curtain, glowering at the outside world. "I understand you were kidnapped today?"

"Yes," I said nodding and biting my bottom lip. "This guy is rather dangerous and unpredictable. And he won't think twice about killing you, or me for that matter. Are you sure you still want this job?"

"Ma'am, I do this for a living. I've watched women who have had stalkers, they've threatened them and me. I can manage just fine."

"Okay, and you have insurance?"

"Yes," he said, and this mouth curved upward into a mini smile before it vanished. "Oh, before I forget. We retrieved your car from the auto pound and your cellphone and wallet was still in your handbag. My team is checking the contents making sure Travis didn't install anything unsavory. You should get your belongings tomorrow morning the latest."

"Thanks," I said and sat at the kitchen counter. I'd completely forgotten about my handbag and now that I thought about it, it was quiet without my cellphone.

Glancing up at the clock, it was almost seven. Travis would be arriving at his apartment to find me gone. I could only imagine how upset he would be and what he would do —perhaps tear the place apart, set it on fire, kill someone. I didn't want to think about it so I turned back to face the kitchen. I should probably make dinner, but I wasn't hungry. There was a heaviness set in the pit of my stomach, either from the drug he'd used on me or the thought of being kidnapped and escaping. I was making light of the entire situation while Donnie and James were here but now that I sit and think about it, that was a close call. That by some chance I had managed to escape, and I was still okay kind of. The heaviness of being taken so easily by Travis was unsettling. I didn't even have the chance to fight him off, I had walked straight into him—literally—and that's all I remembered. Travis knew I was watching him. He must have had the properties on either side to his under watch as well. Or Travis had seen my car parked alongside the road.

I chewed on my fingernail as I rehashed the afternoon. If I didn't escape, I would still be stuck at that apartment and be there for him when he opened the door. I shuddered and stood and walked around the kitchen island and opened the fridge. I stared at the contents of what was inside and closed the door again. We had menus for various restaurants and as much as I needed to eat, I didn't feel like it. "Are you hungry?" I asked, lifting the menus for Wayne to see.

"Sure."

We ordered sushi and burgers. I couldn't make up my mind what I wanted, and I felt like eating both. But when the food arrived, Wayne gave the delivery guys a heart attack each when he drew his weapon and frisked them. He did give them a generous tip each as compensation for man handling them. I pushed my sushi in the soy sauce and finally ate the soggy piece. The burger smelled wonderful, but my stomach was twisted in knots and I wasn't hungry. Wayne noticed but didn't say anything.

Wayne sat at the kitchen island while I watched tv, but all I did was stare at the screen not at the actual actors. I couldn't remember what was on, but I switched it off. It was 8 p.m. Travis would've been at his apartment already; seen I wasn't there and left. Was he outside keeping an eye on me? Was he angry? Of course he was angry, I'd escaped. I'd evaded his torture chamber.

"I can see what's going on all over your face." Wayne said to comfort me, but I did not feel comforted. "I don't sleep much and usually stay up during the night. If I do sleep, I wake easily." It was reassuring but also not. I felt dizzy and wanted to throw up. My eyes pricked with tears which I dusted away with the back of my hand. I smiled uncomfortably at Wayne, silently thanking him for the words. "I didn't want to tell you before in case you freaked out about that, but because of your situation, James hired two of us." That caught my attention, I glanced up at Wayne with surprised eyes; he smiled. "If anyone comes here my guy will see him first and take care of the situation before he can step inside this house. I will also know if anything happens to my guy, we each wear a device we can trigger that warns the rest of us as well as our company of any danger."

"You've clearly had clients in similar situations."

Wayne's smiled brightened his dark eyes and he was actually quite handsome when he wasn't serious and broody. I supposed men in these types of jobs had to give off the impression that they were mean and untouchable. When Wayne realized he was smiling it disappeared quickly and cleared his throat. "We have, so you are in safe hands." He stood and did another sweep of the house.

Chapter Thirteen

TRAVIS

THE ALARM for next door sounded. I approached the cabinet with the monitors and pulled the other side open to view what had happened to activate them. I'd bought both houses on either side of mine because I did not want neighbors peering into my back garden. I preferred my privacy, and even though there were other places I could afford with more space, I liked the area more. The alarm had tripped when the side gate opened a second time this week. The last time that had happened, I was in the bathroom, and when I had checked it, I saw the person had already left. I rewound the tape and saw it was Dana; I'd recognized that dark hair and body anywhere. This time I would catch her in the act, and, if I didn't do this properly, I wouldn't get another opportunity like this ever again. She came gift wrapped for me, and I couldn't help but smile to myself with a warm fuzzy feeling and couldn't wait to unwrap her.

She would be mine.

I grabbed my bag and headed for the side door that led next door. I'd installed various soundproof passages so no one could hear my arrival. With the cloth full of chloroform, I saw her, opened the door quietly and stood behind her.

She didn't hear me approach. She didn't know I was here.

My packaged was waiting to be unwrapped.

All I wanted to do was touch her.

I leaned forward to smell her chestnut-colored hair, sleek and silky, and breathed her in. Before I had a chance to grab her, she turned and walked straight into me; her hands reflexively touched my chest, her mouth parted open in surprise, but she didn't look up. Today really was my lucky day. I slapped the cloth on her face, and she collapsed in my arms. I may have used a bit too much because she fell immediately. I dropped the cloth to the floor so I could hold her in both arms. I steadied her and held her close to my body. Leaning closer, I smelled her sweet scent—florals. Smiling to myself, I returned to my house, kicked open the front door and placed her on the back seat of the Merc. She would be asleep for a few hours, and by that time, she would be safely in my apartment.

After locking the house, I climbed into my car and drove to the apartment block near the company. I owned the apartment block and had refurbished the top bachelor pad into my private holding cell. I'd had only one other woman there, but she was long gone. I kept it empty for Dana while I waited for the right time.

Using my private elevator, I stopped at the top floor with Dana in my arms. Her mouth hung open as she dreamed of nothing. I pulled her closer to feel her breath against my cheek; even though it was slow, it was steady. I pulled the keycard from my pocket and held it against the device on the wall, the door clicked and opened automatically.

I gently placed Dana on the bed with her head on the pillow. I sat beside her and watched. Her chest rose and fell, her soft delicate breasts moving up and down as she slept. Her shirt had ridden up her waist while I had carried her, so I gently pulled it down. My fingers burned to touch her skin, but she needed to be awake. I wanted her to want me as much as I wanted her, and I wanted her to feel my warmth. I removed her hair out of her face, and her skin felt soft and delicate beneath my fingers. I leaned forward, and her warm lips grazed mine, and I allowed myself this one small prize—a kiss. A stolen kiss from the one person who was my soul mate, someone who I knew was my equal. She lay motionless, unknowing, and it made me feel dirty and unwanted. Unloved. It wasn't how I expected it to be; a kiss was something personal and intimate and expressed how one felt for the other, but that stolen kiss did not feel right. I wanted Dana to look me in the eyes to see how much I loved her and how much I cared. Kissing someone drugged did not do it for me.

I left her a note on the bedside table; it would be the first thing she saw when she awoke. It was a waste of my time to stay here until then. I had things to prepare for and would bring dinner with me.

I'd hired a contractor to install a new cage at the compound, told them it was for a wild animal I'd purchased and would be arriving soon. The last occupant had broken three bars and had escaped the cage but not the compound. Luckily, Mr. Maroon saw the little devil escape and threw one of his knives, hitting him in the back. Mr. Bronze used his compound bow on him, and it went through his neck. Suffice to say, he did not make it past the shed.

ONCE I WAS DONE at the compound, I picked up dinner —Chinese, her favorite—and went straight to the apartment block. Taking the private elevator again, I went to my bachelor pad and scanned the keycard, and the door opened to an empty room. I dropped the food and entered, first checking behind the door, the closet, then the bathroom. She had nowhere else to hide in the small pad. The bedside table that should be on the right-hand side was on the floor on the other side and upside down. Glancing up, I saw the window was open.

"Nooo!" I screamed my fury and drove my fist into the plaster wall, leaving a gaping hole beside the closet. She had escaped; I should have known. My knuckles were pink as I drove both fists through the wall, leaving two more holes. The knuckles on my right hand bled, but there was no pain; I didn't feel anything except for rage. It was my mistake. I should have stayed until she woke up. I should have been here. The only way to keep her was to have an eye on her all the time.

I washed my hands and watched the blood disappear down the drain. I was stupid to believe she would want to stay. Stupid to think she wanted me as much as I wanted her. She came to my house; she was actively seeking me out. She wanted me but not the way I'd envisioned. I would bolt the window and bring her back here. She could try escape again. Perhaps the only reason why she sought me out was to have me arrested again. I'd left her alone, thinking she would come around; she might want to stay but she left me.

These four months, I'd left little breadcrumbs for her to find to help make her see I wasn't a bad person, that I had a reason for every kill. They had all been bad people who had to see the evil in their ways. It was not me who had started this, but I was the one to end it. But it didn't help, she had still escaped.

She did not want to be with me. It saddened me to think the only way to keep her was to treat her like I had all the others.

I collected the food from the floor, threw it in the trash, closed the door and went to my car. I knew she would only go to one of two places, unless she went to a hotel and rented a room for the night. She wouldn't go to her parents for fear I would hurt them.

I stopped outside James's house, and it was bathed in darkness. The car moved at a snail's pace past his house, then I drove to the end of the street and turned around. As I eased past his house again, I was confident she wasn't there.

I headed toward her house and saw the lights were on. I noticed a blue car with one occupant who suspiciously scanned the area. I drove to the end of the street, turned around and drove past again. The occupant glanced at a man walking his dog but didn't see me. Her house was alive; her lights were on and, although she'd escaped my apartment, I was elated to know she'd returned home—there really was no place like home. And, as much as I wanted her in my home, it wasn't meant to be. But that didn't mean I couldn't have her for a short while.

I drove around the block and down her street again but parked at the end and behind other cars. The street was dark but alive with people coming home from work, most likely settling in for the evening. When it was safe to climb out of my car, I approached with caution. I wanted to see who that man was and if he was important or not. I traversed the footpath that ran along the edges of the houses and watched the area for any movement.

The rhythm of the night swirled around as I felt the vibrations deep inside of me come alive. This was what I reveled in—the chase, the hunt, the night. I felt the excitement at my fingertips, like electricity coursing through my veins. The mere thought of what my hands were capable of doing and what they longed to do thrilled me.

I caught movement behind her curtains and smiled. I would be with her soon enough. I focused on who sat in that car because I didn't need another threat. I didn't need someone blocking me from what I truly wanted. The muted lullabies and the beat of my heart filled my ears as the drumming vibrations surrounded me; the continuous night sounds soothed my soul. This was my happy place. The dark wind and starless evening called to me so intimately.

The man in the blue Chevy Malibu was busy on his phone; he was muscular and about to lose his patience with whoever he was chatting with on the phone. His appearance screamed security and his presence obvious—someone to guard the house and to keep her safe. As I watched him, I realized it would be too easy. He was on his phone, sending texts then speaking to someone. He rarely glanced up and surveyed the area—he was not doing his job. He was not protecting my Dana. As angry as that made me, I was glad, because I didn't have to work too hard.

No other cars were on the road, nor were there any pedestrians; everybody was inside their homes. His window was wide open, and he was sweating even though the evening air was cool. I approached his window. He said goodbye to the person on the other end. As he glanced at me, I shoved my hand into the window and drove my knife into his throat before he could think to lower his phone or stop me. With my knife lodged in his neck, I pulled it to the side, slicing open his jugular and revealing his spine. He made a *gah* sound, blood sprayed over my hand and down his shirt, and his head lulled to the other side.

Wiping my knife on a clean part of his shirt, I walked around the car and opened the passenger side and climbed in. Papers were everywhere; it was a pigsty—empty food wrappers and juice boxes. I cringed when I saw the dirty steering wheel. This guy most likely ate while he drove.

I grabbed the folder that read *Dana Mulder* on the front seat and tsk-ed the dead guy, flicked him on the forehead, and his head bobbed up and down. He made it so obvious he worked for a security company Dana or her brother had hired to watch over her. He was young, dumb, and that was about it—all muscle and no common sense. I doubted he had been on the team for very long, and it served him right for getting killed the way he had. He was terrible at protecting people. Being distracted on the phone could get you killed.

Opening the folder revealed a one-page printed copy of Dana's address and name, that was it. Closing the folder again, I climbed out the car, checked the area to ensure I was still alone then crossed the street.

Chapter Fourteen

BY 9 P.M., I kept falling sleep on the couch. The chloroform Travis had used on me must be taking its toll on my body. I felt irritated, tired, and miserable. I showered, said good night to Wayne and sent James a text letting him know I was sleeping. He said he would come to my house tonight, but the way I felt, I couldn't stay up waiting for him. The moment my head hit the pillow, I slept.

What felt like only two minutes of sleep was interrupted when glass broke somewhere in the kitchen or living room followed by a gunshot. Feeling disorientated, I sat upright, trying to understand if what I heard was real or if I had dreamt it. My vision was a little fuzzy as I focused on the dark shadows. I heard footsteps running to my room, then all I saw was the gloomy silhouette of a man in the door-jamb. He was too small to be Wayne, and he carried himself like someone I'd seen before in a similar light—*Pighead*. My skin crawled. A coldness traveled through my veins, and I froze. Travis was here and in my house; he'd managed to get through tough security with ease.

He stepped inside my room.

I pulled the covers to my chin, wide awake now.

He stalked farther into my room, and my flight or fight instinct kicked in, but I was frozen to the bed. He stopped when he reached the foot of the bed and stared down at me.

I couldn't see much, but I felt his dark gaze.

"You left me." His face was still bathed in darkness, but the sound of his voice sent a familiar shiver up my spine, not in a good way.

"I'm not yours to keep, Travis." I was feeling brave in that second. He knew I was aware of his name, and to say it out loud and to him was a shock to my system, and it made my nightmare real. After I said his name, he flinched while my body trembled with the unknown sinking feeling of what came next. He was going to hurt me, and there was no turning back. I'd escaped him, and there was no way he would let me get away a second time.

A low rumbling chuckle came from the dark shadow beside me, and I crawled to the other side of the bed, trying in vain to get away from him.

"There's a team of security outside, and they will come in here and kill you. I suggest you leave while you still can," I said as I caught my breath, but it wasn't helping. The bravado I'd felt moments ago was long gone.

He roared with laughter and approached. "That's cute," he whispered. "They're all dead, Dana." The apparent *we know what we are doing security company* was no longer employed, and I was alone—again.

The last thing I remembered was him lunging at me, hitting my head, then darkness.

Chapter Fifteen

FRIDAY

AND THAT'S how I found myself in a cage on a Friday evening instead of being at home and waiting for James. I'd slept the entire day in a cage—or rather I was drugged and left to sleep it off. I turned toward his voice, rubbing my arms for warmth. "You!" I scowled at the figure before me.

His face lit up when he smiled, revealing perfect teeth. "And you never suspected."

"I trusted you."

He laughed sinisterly.

"I told you everything about myself." I folded my arms across my chest.

He cleared his throat. "I must apologize for deceiving you, but it was the only way I could get close enough to you. You were already so scared of me I didn't want to make your fear worse—no matter what you believe."

Now I understood why he had never tried to go after me again these last four months, when before he'd assaulted and shot at me. It was all just a ploy to get closer to me, so close I had confided in him—told him my fears, my wants, and even my fantasies. I cringed inwardly. Not wanting to show how I really felt, I stared at him deadpan.

He gestured to the surroundings. "And sorry about the accommodation, but"—he shrugged nonchalantly—"you needed to be punished and it's the only way to keep you here. After the last time you escaped, I had to make sure you couldn't get away from me again." He neared so I could take in the full effect of the light as it revealed his face.

"I didn't know you were a doctor as well," I said with hate behind each word. For months, I'd been seeing him, telling him how I felt, what scared me, and what I would do if Pig-head ever came after me again—or rather Travis, the soul sucking man before me. And he had sat there and had tried to help me. It was either an ego thing he had going on or he was crazier than I thought—a complete wacko.

"No, but I'd seen enough shrinks during my life to know what to say, how to say it and mean it," Travis said through Dr. Adams's lips. His striking green eyes beneath dark eyelashes shone with the light, and his smile broadened, brightening his face.

I still hated him for what he had done.

"The real Dr. Adams was cremated four months ago and closed his practice." I must've given him a look because he added quickly, "Not me mind you, it was pure luck. Although,"—he pointed to the building in the distance—"that building over there does the job for us. Haven't you ever wondered why there hasn't been any bodies, Dana. After that night, we cleaned up our act and made sure we weren't discovered again." He reached for me.

I backed away so he couldn't touch me.

"I'm sorry I hurt you. You do know that, right?"

I didn't answer him. My hands ached as I squeezed them into fists.

"I said I didn't mean to hurt you, Dana. The least you could do is acknowledge me."

"I do, Travis. The last four, five years, I've done nothing but try to get away from you. You are a killer, and you made me your target. I don't appreciate stalkers—"

"I'm not a stalker, Dana. I stopped going after you when you started seeing me, *professionally*." He smirked.

My laugh came out strangled and sarcastic. "You're sick, you know that?" Perhaps that was the wrong thing to say to someone who wanted to lock me in a cage and most likely kill me, but I'd had enough. "I'm sorry you lost your parents and had a shitty childhood in a mansion. But you aren't the only person to lose someone. Others have gotten on just fine without having to go on a crazy killing spree."

"I help the system, Dana." He kept saying my name as if he loved how each A rolled off his tongue.

I shuddered.

"The criminals who fell through the cracks and were about to hurt more innocent people were never going to be rehabilitated. As far as I'm concerned, I did humanity a favor—"

"I'll be sure to thank you for your service then, but you can stop now." I sounded as cocky as I felt. If he was going to hurt me, at least I would have my say.

He harrumphed and paced, pointing a finger at me. "It's blasé attitudes like that, that will get you killed."

"What do you want?" I asked, getting sick of the banter with a serial killer. We would talk in circles until we were old and gray. I wanted to know what he really wanted.

My words caught his attention, and he grabbed the bars, white knuckling them, and stuck his face between the two he gripped. His sinister features animated in the shadows. "You, Dana. From that first night I laid eyes on you, all I've ever wanted was you. And since you didn't want to stay in my apartment, I had to bring you here. I know for a fact you can't escape this." He glanced up as did I.

The bars reached about eight feet with a bar at the top to connect them—no roof or ceiling, just the night sky. The bars were metal and, without any tools, impossible to bend. The ground beneath me was cement, so I couldn't dig my way out nor climb out. I was caged.

"You have me. Now what? If you are planning on killing me, just get it over and done with. I'm tired of playing this game. I've been scared of you for almost five years, looking over my shoulder every time I went outside, and I've had enough. Just kill me already." I lowered my arms so my hands dangled at my sides and dropped my shoulders to show I was defeated.

He grinned. Sadistic bastard. "As tempting as it is to put a bullet between your eyes, I want more than that. I want a … relationship—"

I burst out laughing, cutting off his words.

He glowered at me, and I stopped, biting my bottom lip instead.

I recalled the images of that biker who had his ankle crushed and every bone in his hands broken then of Eugene's skeletal remains who had suffered a similar fate. As brave as I felt, it would dissolve the moment he took a sledgehammer to my ankle. But, at the same time, I wasn't going to give in.

"That sounds ridiculous. Do you understand why I would never be in a relationship with you?" He was crazier than I thought. His definition of a relationship was warped and unrealistic.

He stared at me with a blank expression that made my arms pebble; he was livid. "Yes, I would see how you would think it was ridiculous, but, if I didn't feel this way about you, you would've been dead four years ago."

My smile melted off my face, and the cold wind chilled me to the bone. I hugged myself against the elements.

"I don't want to hurt you. There were so many times I could've done worse to you." He glanced at my cheek.

Instinctively, I reached for the scar.

"I wanted to do so much more to you," he said almost seductively. "But I wanted to wait for the right moment. I wanted to get to know you first, hence the ruse by pretending to be Dr. Adams, and it was the best decision of my life. I understand you, Dana. I know what you really want. I know what you truly need. My only hope, in time, you will forgive me for what I'd put you through. It hurt me that you were so scared of me. It wasn't what I wanted. I thought it was a game you enjoyed playing, but when you came into the office so distraught, I knew I had messed up and wanted to make it right. I really do want to make things right. Will you give me a chance?"

I swallowed my words. I had nothing to say after that. My body felt numb as I stared at him.

"Well?" he repeated.

Chapter Sixteen

MY LEFT WRIST was bound to the chair and each ankle strapped to a leg. We sat at the table while a waiter dressed in a suit brought our food. Travis wore a navy-blue tailored suit while I was still in my jeans, top, and boots. I had to eat with my fingers. As much as I wanted to refuse the food, I hadn't eaten in over twenty hours, and the nausea from the drugs wouldn't subside until I had a bite to eat. I'd slept in that cage for most of the day and only woke an hour ago, it was 8:49 p.m., and I was starving. Apparently, Travis had waited all evening for me to wake so we could enjoy dinner together.

I hated the man sitting across from me. He'd made my life a living hell for almost five years, and he sat there, beaming like he'd won the golden ticket. He'd scared me, scarred me by leaving his mark on my face, along my jawline, and had sent me a pig's heart. He was a killer, sadist, and frankly unstable. For some reason, he'd kept me alive even after I'd escaped his apartment, and I needed to tread carefully—I knew what he was capable of, and he had left me alive for some reason.

During our sessions, if I could call it that, he had been so put together and sane. But the longer I stared at him, the more I realized I couldn't and shouldn't push his buttons—but it was hard not to.

The waiter didn't dare steal a glance in my direction. I suspected Travis had given him a stern warning to only serve the food, get lost while we ate, and shut up ... or else. Knowing this man, the waiter probably feared his threats were all too real.

"Are the shrimps to your liking?" Travis asked, spearing one with his fork.

"Hmm, it would be better if I didn't have to lick my fingers after each bite." I said and slowly licked my fingers. The last finger I licked was my middle finger, and I kept it in the air so he understood what I meant.

He cleared his throat. "Well, do you blame me? I could always lick them for you?"

I groaned. "No, it's fine."

"Besides, I suspect you would turn a fork into a weapon and use it on me."

I grinned and picked up another shrimp, ate it slowly then licked my fingers again while trying to look bored and left my middle finger for last.

When I finished my shrimp starter, the waiter entered to retrieve our plates.

"Thanks, Mikey." Travis slapped his back. "Mikey is part of my family."

The poor boy glanced at me then nervously averted his eyes.

"His family has worked for mine for years. I watched

them grow up," Travis added when Mikey left with the dirty dishes.

Now I understood the dynamics and why poor Mikey was here. I had to admit he didn't look comfortable being here. Unless me being strapped to a chair made him nervous.

"Do you always introduce your bound dinner guests to family?"

Travis silently poured himself a glass of wine, and I declined his offer. "It's not laced," he said and drank from his glass.

"I haven't had wine since you carved into my face." I held my head high. I would not let him see how he had affected me ... again.

Travis sat back in his chair. His expression was like I'd slapped his face. It was true; I couldn't drink wine after *that* day.

"I truly am sorry for that." He exhaled and sat straight in his chair. "I was angry, and I took it out on you. I wanted to get your attention."

"Well, you got it for sure. But I have to understand why though? I hadn't heard from you for almost four years." I had to find out why he had left me alone for so long only to reveal himself in such an aggressive and violent manner.

"I was watching you from a distance, Dana."

No wonder I felt as though someone had been watching me those years—because someone had been watching me. And again, he said my name like it was the best thing ever. It grated against my skin to hear him say my name that way, like he enjoyed every letter rolling off his tongue—slow, seductive, and careful.

"I watched you every single day. I followed you wherever you went. I saw how you worked and what you did. I wanted to get to know the real Dana, not from reading about you on a screen—I wanted to know the real you. What made you laugh, cry, and angry. I was waiting for the perfect opportunity to be with you, and unfortunately, things changed because of James. When I noticed he had an interest in you, I had to stop it. I guess if I couldn't have you, nobody else could."

"You do realize you drove me into James's arms?"

"I did make it worse, yes. I see the fault in my plan. Although I could tell he wanted you from the first time he met you. Then the following Sunday, he was with Donnie for lunch with your parents, and he couldn't take his eyes off you."

The hairs on the back of my neck stood on end.

"Travis—"

Mikey burst through the door with the main meal—a steak with mashed potatoes and vegetables. My steak was cut into bite size blocks, with a plastic spoon for the potatoes.

"Thanks, Mikey," I said when he placed the plate before me.

"You were saying?"

"I don't know how to say this nicely, so I'll just say it. You and I can never be together."

Travis's lip twitched, and he set down his knife and fork. He placed his elbows on the table and steepled his fingers. "Oh, I realized that, Dana. Don't worry about my delicate sensibilities. I'm not an imbecile."

"I didn't think you were, but you're doing all this for nothing." I waved my free hand at the table and the food on top.

"I know. Think of this as your last supper." His lip twitched again and smiled unnaturally. He sliced through his bloody steak and chewed. Red juice splashed onto his plate, a stark contrast against the white.

A nervousness I'd never experienced before settled in my chest, but everything felt strange. Travis was like a yoyo —one moment, he wanted a *relationship* of sorts; the next it's my last supper. I glanced outside at the outline of the building he had indicated where he incinerated bodies then at the bloody steak on his plate.

"But"—he continued speaking while he chewed—"you could always persuade me from cutting your life short."

I choked on the meat, leaned forward and spat it out or I would've died laughing. "What does that mean?"

He arched an eyebrow. "What do you think it means? You aren't stupid, Dana." There, again, he said my name sweetly and seductively yet menacingly. "Either this is your last dinner, ever, or you can change my mind for me—in my bedroom." He sliced through his steak but kept a watchful eye on me. "And I want you to want it."

Suddenly, I lost my appetite and sat back in the chair. My left wrist itched, so I stuck my finger under the cable ties and scratched but not quite getting there. Travis was toying with me, pulling me one way only to jerk me in the opposite direction.

He finished his steak as Mikey entered the dining area to collect our plates—either he kept an eye on us or Travis had a way of informing him when to bring the next course.

If I was about to die in the next couple of hours, the least I could do was get a couple of answers out of him. And, from his demeanor, I didn't think it would be a problem.

"Do you remember the night your parents were killed?"

He leaned back in his chair and didn't answer me for at

least a full minute, he just stared at me and narrowed his eyes. "You want to know more about me?"

I nodded.

"Fine, I guess I owe you that. You probably know about my baby sister. I know you've been digging."

"Yes, I found out about the third DNA sample from when your parents were murdered."

"Eugene worked for my father one summer at Devil Mountain. He did the handiwork around the house and even tended to the garden. One weekend, my father was away on a business trip, and he and my mother got busy, and the obvious happened. Whether my mother allowed it to happen on purpose, I will never know. My father realized what had happened when he found out the gestational age of the baby and knew he was out of town around that time. That was part of the reason why I killed Eugene." He slowly sipped from his wine, glaring at me over the rim of the glass. "The worst was when I did something my father didn't like—bounce my ball in the house, break a vase by accident, or simply walking past while he was in a business meeting—he would lash me. I'd be bent over his desk in his office while Eugene and my mom watched, and they did nothing to stop it. Only when my father saw blood through my clothing did he stop. I learned quickly how to tune out the pain, to listen to the rhythm of my heart, to hear the quiet of the night or my slow, steady breathing. If I didn't feel anything, maybe my father wouldn't keep doing it. But he didn't stop. And as much as I appreciated Eugene for what he did for me, I hated him more for taking away my sister. He took away the one thing I wanted—family who didn't hurt me. And I wanted to protect her. But I couldn't."

I shifted uncomfortably in his stare, unable to respond to his childhood trauma. However, I could understand what he had experienced at such a young age was enough to do some kind of permanent damage. I really could see how it had scarred him for the rest of his life. Unfortunately, revenge was not the answer, it just meant a void he could never fill.

"And that's why I did what I did. All those people were bad. Not one didn't deserve what happened to them—"

"What about Nigel? He was a good man. You helped to solve his family's murder, yet you tricked him and killed him in the end."

"Nigel was not who you thought he was, Dana. Nigel was a *ghost* who killed more innocent people than guilty. He was the worst of them. He did try and change when he worked for Marc, but he still did side jobs where the highest bidder won."

I frowned. "What does that mean?"

"Nigel was a gun for hire, Dana. He killed for a living, even children."

I snorted my disgust and disbelief. "That's ridiculous. He would never."

Travis produced a tablet and tapped on the screen. He turned around the device and showed me a picture of Nigel leaving the scene of a crime where an entire family had been murdered. "This was taken three weeks before his death." The next picture showed Nigel lifting his arm, holding a hammer, and blood over the wall and on a man in bed. "This was last year."

"Okay, enough." I felt sick to the core, not because of the gruesome scenes but because it was Nigel. The pictures didn't seem to be altered; it was Nigel doing those things. If Marc knew about Nigel's actions, I couldn't continue to work with him.

"I have more, Dana. I do not *take* lives lightly. Every

single one of our hunts all deserved what they got. Nigel was no different."

"Did Marc know?"

"No, he didn't. Marc is a good guy. If he wasn't, he would've been gone long ago."

I swallowed, and the back of my throat ached. I knew I didn't know everything about Nigel, but what he did was awful, unthinkable, and disgusting. I couldn't believe it.

"I can see that you can't understand how could Nigel do that and why. But he was a trained killer, Dana. I must admit he did try to leave after his family's death, but he continued when he couldn't solve their murder. It's a chicken and egg story, unfortunately. Would he have continued if they had lived? Maybe. Would he have continued if he found their killer at the time? Maybe. Somethings we will never know."

The silence stretched between us. It was a lot to process. I'd worked with someone for four years yet knew nothing about them. I hated to admit it and wouldn't out loud, but Travis made sense, but it was still wrong.

"Would you like to know about James?"

"No!" I yelled and shook my head. "I don't want to know."

"Are you sure?"

"Yes! Please do *not* tell me."

"What about your brother?"

"No!" I narrowed my eyes at him. If James or Donnie had done something, I would rather hear it from them, not from a killer.

"Fine." Travis switched off the tablet and placed it on the chair beside him. "Do you have any more questions?"

I was emotionally spent and knew enough about Travis and his family. I didn't want to know any more, especially secrets about the people I cared for. "No, I've got nothing left to say." I exhaled and slumped in the chair, the cable ties cutting into my wrist, and whimpered. "Please, can you loosen this? It's hurting me."

Travis considered my request and walked around the table. His left hand held my hand and gently pulled it down while his other produced a large hunting knife. He slipped the cold blade between my wrist and the cable tie and easily cut through it. My hand was free of the cable tie but not his hand. He pointed the sharp knife near my face. "I won't hesitate to use this on you again if you try to escape."

It would be difficult if I tried. My ankles were tied to the legs of the chair and would need to grab his knife in order to cut myself free.

"I won't." A red welt formed on top of my wrist which I rubbed for comfort.

"Good, then we can enjoy the rest of our meal."

For dessert, we had cheesecake, which was delicious. I finished mine before Travis was halfway through his. The rest of the meal was in silence, which I preferred; I had nothing I wanted to say to Travis. But I did think about his offer. The mere thought of following him to his bedroom, allowing him to touch my body and to do it willingly, made me gag. I doubted he would let me go even if I did do that.

Mikey served coffee and cookies, freeing me of my dark thoughts, and I knew I had to say something before we ended the meal.

"I've been thinking about your offer. Thanks, but I don't think I will be joining you in your room."

"As you wish, Dana. It would be a great loss. You don't know what you're missing. But I will take great joy and comfort that you made the decision yourself. And that you are aware of the consequences because of it."

I swallowed the lump in my throat. "Will I be sleeping out there again?" I glanced outside. I was ready to sleep under the stars, but one last night on a bed wouldn't hurt. My body still ached from climbing out that window and trying to fight off Travis.

"No, you can enjoy your last night on one of my beds," he said with a smirk. He didn't say which of his beds, but I would make damn sure the door locked. "Are you finished?"

I downed the rest of the coffee and nodded.

"Mikey will take you to the room."

Just like magic, Mikey approached me.

Travis stood, came around the dining table and held his knife to my throat. "Any sudden movements while he cuts your legs free and I will take great joy watching you bleed over my floor."

Chapter Seventeen

MIKEY BROUGHT me to a room on the ground floor already fitted with a manacle and chain connected to the wall. Mikey crouched near my feet and placed the manacle around my left ankle with shaky hands and closed it. He gently stuck his finger between the manacle and my ankle, ensuring it wasn't too tight.

We were alone while Travis was upstairs in his office. I needed help escaping, and even though he had said Mikey was like family, did he approve of Travis's behavior?

"Does Travis do this often?" I whispered when Mikey tugged on the cold metal bracelet around my ankle.

He shushed me and stood. "You don't want him angry."

"I know he's crazy. Please, can you help me?" My words were barely a whisper. "He's going to kill me." I pleaded with teary eyes.

Mikey opened his mouth to respond when Travis's words echoed in the passage, making me flinch. "What's taking so long, Mikey? Do you need me to help you?"

Although Travis was teasing, it felt like a double-edged sword.

"No, it's fine. I was just testing the chain."

"Good boy." Travis poked his head around the door-jamb and arched an eyebrow. "Are you sure nothing's going on? It looks like something is going on here. Mikey? Why are you standing so close to her?" Travis entered the room and glowered down at Mikey.

"I tested the chain and then stood, Travis." Mikey grabbed Travis's elbow. "Are we having that drink before we sleep?" He released Travis and exited the room.

My hope died a miserable death when Mikey left.

Travis stared hungrily at me, and I shivered. He leaned against the closet, folded his arms across his broad chest and looked fixedly at me.

I wanted to cower or hide away; it was such an intense gaze that I instinctively stepped backward—which only made him smile more.

"Tonight, I will allow you to rest. I promise not to come inside your room—unless you want me to?"

I shook my head.

"Suit yourself." He didn't move, he just stared down at me. "Tomorrow, the others will come, and I will introduce you. They're a great bunch of people. Then before sundown, we will hunt you," he said like it was something normal people did every day, like doing the dishes or washing laundry and not killing someone.

I swallowed hard, and the back of my throat ached.

When he realized I had nothing to say, he pushed himself away from the closet. "I'm sorry, but I have to do it." Then he lunged at me. He gripped my face with his hands like a vise, pulled me to him and kissed me.

I pushed against him, but he was much stronger. His lips

were soft against mine as I kept my mouth closed and my lips tight. I pushed against his chest even though the pressure felt as though it would squash my face.

"No!" I managed to say and kicked his shin. When he released me, I slapped him.

He howled in laughter.

I backed up, afraid he would hit me back, but he didn't.

He wiped his mouth and pointed a finger at my chest. "I'll let that one go, but hit me again and I'll break your ankle. It will be incredibly hard and painful for you to run with only one good leg." He smirked knowingly.

I hugged my body and stepped farther away from him.

He shook his head. "I wanted to give you a chance, I really did, but you make it incredibly hard for me to do that. And I'm sorry to say this, but, if I can't have you, nobody can." He turned on his heel and closed the door behind him, locking it.

Sitting on the bed, I stared at the door, waiting for him to come back and finish the job—to just shoot me. When he didn't return, I made sure the door was locked and pushed the chair against the door. If he entered while I slept, I would hear him and give me a head start to protect myself.

I used the bathroom, washed my hands and face and sat on the bed again. That distinct feeling of being watched made me glance at the ceiling. The corners of each cornice seemed normal, but that didn't mean monitoring devices weren't hidden somewhere else. He could've inserted cameras in the lamps, headboard, closet—anywhere really —but I couldn't see anything.

Feeling exhausted, I climbed under the covers and switched off the lamp. Lying on my back, I scrunched the bedding close to my body as I stared at the ceiling. My head and body ached. Still feeling disgusted by the kiss, I knew I had to find a way to either kill him or get away. The metal against my ankle was irritating; there was no comfortable way to lie with it.

I kicked my foot against the covers, and the shackle clicked and fell away. I lay motionless, not quite believing, but positive Mikey didn't do such a great job at closing the manacle around my ankle. Perhaps Mikey didn't agree with what his *uncle* was doing—kidnapping a woman and holding her against her will.

I smiled but not for long. If Travis had cameras and saw me smile, he would be suspicious. No woman in her right mind would smile if they were here. I needed to wait until I was sure Travis would be asleep before I attempted to escape. I would rest my eyes for only a moment.

Chapter Eighteen

SATURDAY

STRONG HANDS WERE around my shoulders and shaking me. I heard the words but couldn't understand them. I opened my eyes, and Mikey was above me, still shaking me. I focused on his lips, then I heard his words.

"You were supposed to escape. Why didn't you leave?" he asked as he gripped my shoulders.

"Please stop shaking me." I lifted my arms from underneath the covers to swat his.

He let go and stood backward. "You need to leave before he wakes up," he whispered. "You must believe I had no idea what he was doing. He asked if I wanted to make extra money this weekend, and I knew it would be easy money. I didn't know it would be *this*." He frantically checked the closed door. He wore an expression that frightened me, and I wondered if he was as scared of Travis as I was.

"How did you get in here?" I noticed the chair I'd placed against the door was still there. Glancing at the curtain, I saw it move.

"You still have time to leave, but you must go now. He usually wakes around six, but he's a light sleeper."

"What time is it?"

"Four in the morning." He handed me my shoes, and I pulled them on. "When I first saw you, I couldn't understand why he had tied you to the chair but didn't think it was my place to question him. But when I saw your picture on the news while I was preparing dinner, I knew he had done something. Your face is everywhere. You must know I didn't know what he was planning."

"It's okay, Mikey. I believe you. Have you met any of his other friends before?"

He shook his head.

"It's okay." I squeezed his shoulder for comfort.

"Remember, the walls are smooth on the inside. I never understood why he did it, but I do now," Mikey said with a haunted look. "But there's a way for you to climb over easily."

I pushed the curtain aside.

Mikey stood beside me and pointed to the wall on our left. "You can't see it from here, but on the left, where the wall meets the edge of the house wall, there's a slight dent, as if a brick had moved while it was settling. You can use that as a step and climb over. The wall has electric fencing, but I've switched it off. And take this." He handed me a blanket. "Throw it over before you climb."

"Thank you, Mikey. You've saved my life. You don't want to come with me? If he knows you helped, he will hurt you."

"He won't hurt me. My family has done so much for him. If he hurt me, it would be like hurting his kid brother."

"Are you sure?"

He nodded, but not convincingly.

"My name is Dana Mulder. If you need me, you can look me up. I'm a private investigator."

"I know who you are, Dana, and I will be fine."

In my gut, I didn't believe him. Travis would take his anger out on him when he saw I'd left. As much as I wanted to stay, I knew I had to leave, or this would end badly for both of us. I climbed out of the window and jumped to the ground with the blanket in hand. I glanced left and right; on the right was the cage I was in yesterday, to my left was freedom.

I ran, following the wall to the left, until I came to the high perimeter wall. Just as Mikey had said, I saw an indent into the wall where I could put my foot and climb over. First, I threw the blanket over the electric fence and nothing sparked. Then I placed my foot in the indent and scaled the wall, gripped the blanket and fence, and I didn't sizzle. I flung my left leg over then my right, and I sat on the wall for a second to catch my breath.

Glancing over my shoulder, I saw Mikey outside of the window of the room I had slept in, and he shooed me away. A light came on upstairs. I gripped the fence and spun around. The ground on the other side was more than six feet away. If I jumped off, I was sure to break both ankles. Yelling echoed from inside the house. Mikey was gone. The faint sound of buzzing started. I slowly swung my other foot over and leaned on my elbows. I gripped the blanket as I dropped to the ground, falling into a rose bush. I bit my lip and tongue, that twangy metal taste erupted in my mouth as I released a silent scream. The blanket fell on my head, and I pressed my body against the wall and off the roses. Thorns stuck out of my tender flesh, and I was sure something was in my foot.

Screaming continued from the house as Travis crashed

through the rooms like a Tasmanian devil. I flinched when gunshots went off. The electric fence buzzed alive above me, and I gripped the blanket for dear life.

Hobbling away from the wall, I knew I had to find a phone. I struggled to see in the dark and couldn't decipher any other houses or lights nearby. I glanced back to make sure Travis wasn't following me, but all I saw were the wall and the lights at his house.

I followed the street until I came to a T-junction and went right. I wanted to get away from Travis's house; if I went left, I would've gone straight to his front door. I heard a car rev and speed away. I limped to a bush and hid until I couldn't hear anything besides my breathing. When I was sure I was alone, I continued walking until I found the closest house.

Chapter Nineteen

MR. AND MRS. MANSOOR waited on me like the angels they were. Donnie and James were on their way, bringing the cavalry, while I had a cup of tea. Mrs. Mansoor tended to the thorn in my foot. I'd just scraped my sides when I fell into the rose bushes, and they weren't serious, but I'd stepped onto a cactus, and one of its spines pierced my shoe and entered my heel. I had my leg raised and was biting on a stick, curtesy of Mr. Mansoor, while Mrs. Mansoor removed my shoe and, with tweezers, dislodged the spine. Feeling more like she had removed a bone, my vision blurred, and I gripped the armrest of the chair as she cleaned the area. Once I'd started breathing again, I could see again. Something sounded in the kitchen, and I jumped, almost kicking Mrs. Mansoor in the face.

She tapped my ankle to settle me down. "It's all right, dear. It's just the mister making more tea."

It seemed with every noise, I'd flinch or wanted to jump up and run away. But I was safe here even though it didn't feel like it. Red and blue lights splashed against the curtains, and a sense of relief engulfed me; at least five cars were outside the house.

A moment later, Donnie burst through the door with James hot on his heel.

"I'm okay guys," I said, trying to stand, but Mrs. Mansoor tsk'ed me and told me to sit still.

"Are you sure? Now, where is this place of his?" Donnie asked as he paced.

James came to my side and planted kisses all over my dirty face.

I was sure he tasted sweat, but I didn't care. I held his hand and squeezed as Mrs. Mansoor bandaged my foot.

"What happened?" James asked, jerking his chin at my foot.

"I fell into a garden full of rose bushes and cacti."

"Thank you for helping her," James said, grabbed my shoe and helped me stand once Mrs. Mansoor finished bandaging my foot.

"Thank you. You guys really saved my life." I hugged the Mansoors.

When I had banged on their doors and almost broke it, they had recognized me from the news. They didn't hesitate to help me. They were such a sweet couple, and I hoped Travis didn't find out they had assisted me. I told James they needed protection just in case we didn't find Travis at home.

We left the Mansoors, and I told Donnie where I thought I had walked from. The Mansoors house was on the same road as Travis's, and, after five minutes, we reached his blacked-out house down a hill. Donnie sent two uniforms to knock on the door. They returned, saying nobody was home.

"We have a no-knock warrant. Break down the door!" Donnie yelled.

The two officers returned to their squad car and grabbed the battering ram. They were inside within two minutes with six others behind them, their weapons trained on anything that moved.

Donnie and James waited with me in their car in case Travis came home.

One officer ran toward the car, shaking his head.

"What's up?" Donnie asked.

"Nobody's here, man, but there's another building in the middle of his yard with a smoking chimney. One of the guys is trying to get in, but it has a metal door. We might need to blowtorch it," he said and left.

"Oh no!" I yelled from the back seat.

Both men turned to stare at me.

"That's how I escaped. Mikey helped me, and something tells me that's his body burning."

We couldn't do anything about it; I was too late. I smelled the smoke and cried silently in the dark privacy of the back seat while the place swarmed with police. Mikey had given his life for mine, and he was supposedly *family* of Travis's. The cold and heartless monster had killed that young boy all because I'd escaped. I imagined him doing the same to me once he found me. I doubted Travis would allow me out of his sights for a second should he find me. There was no way I could allow that to happen.

This was it, it had to end now. There was no safe way for me to continue living with Travis still around, or his vigilante killers. If I returned to work like nothing had ever happened, Travis would just keep coming for me again and again until he killed me. I had already refused witness protection, because Travis had access to some of the systems and would know where I was.

He would always know.

Now was the time once and for all to do what I should've done four years ago.

————

Travis

"Why aren't we at the compound, Travis?" Joe lifted his rifle and aimed it at Rex.

"The compound was compromised." I sheathed my knife and grabbed my shotgun. "This is just a temporary solution."

"Shouldn't we lie low?" Aika asked and stood behind Damian.

"I agree. It's dangerous doing this when the cops are after you." Dafne twirled hair between her fingers.

My nostrils flared as I exhaled. "We have to do this today. It is our Saturday hunt, and we always do it on Saturdays. If you don't like it, go stand with Rex." I pointed my shotgun at Dafne and Aika.

"No, it's okay." Dafne raised her hands. "We will hunt."

"It's fine, Travis. We will stay," Aika added quickly.

"Good, because he knows my name now. There's no way we can let him go." I rolled my eyes at Aika and approached the cowering man bound in chains tied to a cement block on the ground. I lifted my weapon and peered down the barrel at Rex. As much as I wanted to pull the trigger, this was Dafne's hunt. "Are you ready, Dafne?"

"It's okay, Travis. You can have it."

"No." I turned to face her. "It's yours."

"I really don't mind. Either you or Joe can have it." She nervously played with her weapons.

"We came all this way to Wolf Road Woods, and you're

telling me you don't want to do it?" My pulse thundered in my ears as the thrumming of those silent drums filled the quiet air. A spider web filled my vision as I lunged at her. My cold hands reached for her and gripped her throat. I laced my fingers around her warm neck and felt a current course through me as I squeezed. "You. Will. Do. It," I said through gritted teeth, spittle dripping off my chin.

Dafne dropped her Glock and knife and tried to pull my hands free from her neck.

"Easy, Travis," Joe said beside me. "She's part of the team, remember. She's one of us. If you hurt her, you're hurting the team. Why don't you let her go, and we can decide who helps her with the hunt? Maybe she's just having an off day and doesn't feel like it today."

It made sense. I knew Joe was right, but I couldn't let go. I couldn't ease my control no matter what I tried. I needed the order we'd had for so many years, yet it was slowly slipping through my fingers. Warm hands gripped mine and pried me off Dafne's throat. The spider web vision dissolved, and her face cleared as I blinked at her.

Dafne's makeup had smudged and stained her cheeks. Her whimpering continued once her neck was free from my grasp.

The constant beat had eased, and I heard the insects around us. I looked my Horsemen in the eyes one by one and knew I'd lost them. I'd attacked one of our own. I'd made a mistake by going after her.

Dafne fell to the ground with Aika and Neal beside her, consoling her.

I grabbed my shotgun, not remembering when I'd dropped it, raised it and pulled the trigger.

Rex's face exploded; bits of brain matter and skull flew in the air as his body dropped to the ground.

I turned, grabbed the camera and tripod and stalked to my Merc.

"Hey, Travis. Where are you going?" Joe called, but I didn't answer.

I climbed into my car and sped away.

ONCE INSIDE MY STUDIO APARTMENT, I connected the camera to the television. I wanted to understand what had happened. It had been going fine until Dafne refused the kill. I watched the footage. The camera had been positioned at the correct angle; I could see Rex's petrified face along with everyone else's. My back was to the camera, but I could see everyone's shocked expressions. Their facades had cracked, splintered, broken when I lunged at Dafne. I paused the video and sipped my whiskey, neat and smooth. I rewound and pressed Play to watch it again. I paused the footage at the right spot. And I saw it again. The shocked expressions they wore were a punch in the gut. Their wide eyes. The distance they stood from me. It all spoke volumes.

None of them wanted to be there.

They didn't want to do this anymore.

They'd lost their nerve.

I'd lost them.

It was over ...

Chapter Twenty

TUESDAY

I WATCHED James and Donnie discuss our strategy, but it was white noise at this stage. They were trying to talk me out of joining them. It had been two days since my second escape, and Travis had disappeared. His house and compound had someone watching for his return. The FBI were watching the house he had converted into a bar. Seekster hadn't heard from Aika nor Travis since Friday, and their cellphones were off. Aika's house hadn't seen any movement since then either.

Captain Dodd and the FBI had joined task teams now that Travis had resurfaced and had a handful of agents working on the case. From what Donnie had told me, the FBI hadn't stopped investigating Travis and had been looking into the deaths of his business partner, Gregory Johnston, and Travis's girlfriend. Gregory had *retired* five years ago and hadn't been seen since; even his ex-wife had been looking for him even though she had received a post-card from Hawaii. Travis's girlfriend, Mia Elliston, had been missing about the same time. Her parents had said they had no idea who she was dating, but all her friends had said it was Travis.

The FBI had also been investigating those responsible for the contracts with Seekster from the various state departments. It seemed they were blackmailed into stepping down, and Travis had paid, under the table, those who took over from them to keep his contract as is so he could maintain his claws in the system. But what Travis hadn't known was he had been given a mirror system to connect his program. The FBI had traced his movements and had built a large file with charges against him. The FBI were waiting for the right moment for when he resurfaced before striking. What they had done was sneaky, but I was happy to know they weren't idiots for keeping him on contract when they suspected his nefarious deeds. How Travis got those contracts in the first place was beyond me. But if I knew Travis as well as I did, he had scandalous information on top people—ready to use and abuse it.

All that was about to come crashing down on him.

With both of my kidnappings, the FBI now had enough evidence against Travis—a witness. They were actively seeking him out and had searched all his properties. They had seized everything on Sunday evening at Seekster— confiscating documents, raiding safes, and interviewing employees. But they left the bar alone. Either one of Captain Dodd's men or an agent in eight-hour shifts were now watching it. They even searched Aika's house on Sunday, but she too had disappeared.

"You're not doing this," James said, pulling me from my thoughts.

"I wouldn't, man," Donnie said, siding with me.

"The only reason the FBI can do this is because of me. Otherwise, they'd still be trying to identify the vigilante killers. The FBI would never know who to look for if it wasn't for me. Travis has ensured their identities remain hidden, but I know what they look like. I can review the cases from four years ago and work our way backward to distinguish them. Then we can decide on our next move. But first, we need to know who they are."

James sighed frustratingly, leering at Donnie for having my back and not his. They were partners, yet Donnie always sided with me. "Okay, but if we are doing this, you listen to us—"

"No. If we are doing this"—I pointed at each of us— "we do it together. I will not be sitting on the sidelines while the two of you have all the fun."

"Dana, this isn't some Girl Scout camping we're about to do."

"Dude, don't go there," Donnie added. "She goes hunting with me and my dad all the time, and she's a great shot."

"I'm not discounting that she's good at what she does—"

"I won't get hurt, James." I smiled knowingly at him. This was it, the crux of his resistance, why he didn't want me to do this with them. He didn't want me to get hurt and didn't want to lose me. He was only frightened at the thought of losing me. I gently pushed Donnie out of the way, and I went to James and wrapped my arms around his waist. "We will be okay if we do this together and look out for each other. For years, they have evaded the FBI and, to some extent, you guys. But I've seen what the others look like. I know who they are. You need me with you." I pressed my chin into his chest and glanced up. "The FBI may have seized assets, but they only know of the two of them. To help them along, Johnny has agreed to give me his copies of the case along with his notes. The FBI is happy for us to continue with our own investigation, just as long as we let them know what we've found." A shudder ran through me at the thought of Travis and his delusions about me and that the only reason I'm still alive was because he liked me. "Copies of Johnny's casefiles were couriered yesterday, and we should get them soon. I've messaged Billie, letting him know the three of us are on our way as soon as we can. He is expecting us, and he is the only one I trust to breach any firewall Travis may have set up."

James kissed the top of my head. "I just don't want you to get hurt ... again."

"I know. But we are together and will keep each other safe."

Chapter Twenty-One

WEDNESDAY

DONNIE'S WIFE Madeline and the three boys had left for a vacation with our parents. We did not know where they were, only it was out of the country. Once we received confirmation from Captain Dodd, we had the go-ahead to do what we needed to. Captain Dodd was the only person who knew of our plans and had agreed to them. Should anything go wrong, he at least knew about it and could inform the FBI.

I was the first to wake and made coffee, filling the house with that wonderful aroma.

James joined me in the kitchen when a knock sounded on the door.

Donnie flew from the room where he had slept with his gun aimed at the door while James grabbed a knife out the block.

I rolled my eyes. "Stand down, cowboys. It's only the mailman." I opened the front door.

The postman handed me the envelope.

I signed, and he left. "It's the casefiles from Johnny." I said, closed the door and sat at the kitchen island. I read through the casefile first. As I finished a page, I handed it to James who, in turn, handed it to Donnie.

We drank our coffee in silence as we absorbed the information. After reading these again after all this time, I thought I would be shaking in a corner somewhere. But strangely enough, my therapy actually helped, even though it was Travis who had offered the advice. I did not want to dwell on the dark thoughts, otherwise it would impact our mission, and too much was at stake to even consider quitting. From where I had been to where I was now was an improvement, and I would gladly thank Travis when I saw him again, with a knife in his heart. Although I wouldn't say that out loud, James wanted to arrest Travis, but Donnie and I were on the same page; we wanted him dead. We both knew the only way he would ever stop doing what he did was if he was gone. No prison would hold a man like that, and I was sure he would find a way not to go. But so many deaths were attributed to his name I wasn't sure he could pull it off.

From my sneaky break in at the health and wellness center and overhearing each member spew their stories during the support session, I could associate each vigilante killer with a particular case—who the loved one was, who had died, and how they related to the victim they had tortured and killed.

Donnie drilled holes into my living room wall and hung the corkboard while I stuck pages from the casefile in order of the victim's deaths. With Post-its, I added the original victims who had died and their family members. We only had names of the vigilante killers and would have Billie assist us with photos of these people and where they lived along with any relevant information he could find on them. As discussed, we did not want to use the police system, for fear of Travis finding out we were on to them. Going behind the scenes was the only way for now, and whether Travis would find out was yet to be seen.

What surprised me the most was the FBI had a string of crime scenes and victims that suggested Travis was involved, but there was no physical evidence or witnesses to charge him. He was only a person of interest, and that's where it ended. I'd never seen this information before, and when I'd questioned Johnny about it, he'd alluded that the FBI did much behind closed doors he wasn't privy to, and that was when he still worked there. And since he only consulted on an ad-hoc basis, he was out of the loop completely. But, with enough arm twisting, he acquired this information for us.

What was interesting was the case reports dated back to 1986. A neighbor had reported Travis who was only five or six at the time. She had accused Travis of killing her cat. The police questioned his parents, and that was it. They didn't contact a social worker or wrote supplemental reports or included witness statements. It was possible his parents settled the dispute directly with the neighbor, which could explain why they moved around quite a bit; they frequented six properties at different times of the year. Travis did not have a proper school education and did not attend any school; he only had tutors. I wondered how the FBI got hold of that piece of information.

I glanced at the victims' names for all the other crimes they associated Travis with, and I didn't recognize any except for Nails; he was part of a biker gang in Chicago.

They had found him killed with a bullet to the head in the woods, his body tortured and broken. I made notes and stuck them on the corkboard, outlining the events and the victims' identities, along with their relatives. I recognized the other victims as part of that case I had worked on four years ago, along with their relatives.

Joseph Slade: his brother Jacob had committed suicide, and they blamed Sam O'Reilly and Kelly Pope for his death. Even though neither men were ever arrested, they did have complaints against them for victimization or harassment, but the police had not brought charges against them. The ME's report highlighted the various wounds on each of their bodies, wounds made with various sharp objects and by both left- and right-handed attackers. A longer blade had pierced their abdomens, almost cutting them in half. One assailant had used a deep serrated hunting knife that ripped gaping wounds into the victims. Even a box cutter had been used to carve patterns into the soft delicate skin around their necks. Staring at the pictures, I thought it looked like someone had carved into a pumpkin, except it was flesh. The ME also found a screwdriver had been used to stab their delicate bellies. At least six perpetrators—four men and two women—had sliced and diced each victim. Sam's and Kelly's bodies had been buried in shallow graves at Washington Park, while their vehicle had been discovered at Jackson Park.

Aika Davids: her husband, Stephen, had been swindled out of his money—all their money—and he continued to drink his problems away with what little money he had left. Someone had attacked him one night outside a bar where they had killed him and left him to die in the gutter with the trash. He may have died poor, but Aika had inherited a handsome amount of insurance, ensuring she lived a wealthy lifestyle for the rest of her days. Which made me wonder why she ever worked at Seekster with Travis. The victim, Wyatt McKlusky, died by a thousand cuts. As per the ME report, his jugular had been severed, and he had bled to death. Again, multiple weapons had been used on his body after his death, each performed by different people. A compound bow had been used on his chest, knife carvings into the back of his neck, a rifle had been used on his stomach, and fragments from a Glock had been found in his legs. On his back, they had found burn marks. Thank heavens he was already dead by then, otherwise it would have been excruciatingly painful. His body had been dumped on Chicago's southside.

Dafne Charles: her husband was Jack. The police had arrested his business partner, Kevin, for his murder, but, after they'd discovered evidence that someone else had gained entrance into the office and had murdered Jack, they had to release Kevin. From what I gathered in the report, complexities had surrounded the contract that sparked their interest in Kevin in the first place. Allegedly, it had been a contract deal gone bad, and Jack had refused to sign over his share of the business to Kevin. But Kevin had denied this and had written in his statement, with accompanying documents, that Jack had wanted to sell his part of the business to travel with his girlfriend. I wondered how Dafne had taken this piece of information or whether she had known all along. Dafne had received millions from his estate while his share of the business had gone to his partner. But because they had accused Kevin of killing Jack, another firm had bought the business. This new firm belonged to Kevin's sister. In the end, Kevin had owned the company with his sister. It was a complicated mess, and I didn't think anyone came out of it the winner. Kevin's body had been found near Riverdale at the Kensington Marsh.

Neal Tipping: his sister had died of a drug overdose, but the ME had ruled it an accident, as she had been home alone. However, the police had arrested her husband, Dylan, for possession of narcotics with intent to sell. They had released Dylan shortly after her death. He had cleaned up and became a model dad to their two kids. Neal and his wife had submitted a request to foster the two kids, which the courts had approved following Dylan's relapse. Dylan's battered and bruised body had been discovered at Big Marsh in Chicago's greater Calumet region, which had been later transformed into a bike park. Dylan's face had received a pummeling—a broken jaw and missing three teeth. He had been strangled, and the ME had noted a crushed larynx and petechial hemorrhaging. The rest of his body had received a similar send off with a bullet in his chest, carvings behind his neck, a bow to the chest, and burn marks.

Damian Brooks: a drunk driver, William, had killed Damian's wife when the driver had skipped a red light straight into her car. She had died on impact, while William had walked away from the scene. William had been a connected man and, after a brief court case, had only attended community service. I sympathized with Damian, I really did, but there must have been other ways to ensure William had received proper punishment. They had been carrying his body down the embankment that night four years ago when we had attacked them, and the vigilante killers had slaughtered all the agents.

The FBI had associated other possible victims with Travis due to the similar knife wounds. A homeless man had been stabbed multiple times in his side and abdomen and had been left to die in the gutter and had only been found when someone had complained about the stink in the area.

Another body had been discovered near the coffee shop Donnie and I always met for lunch. "Donnie!" I yelled and pointed at the victim. "Look where he was found." I pointed at the dumpster alley where Donnie had been struck and left bleeding.

Donnie's eyes widened, and he cleared his throat. "That's the asshole who shot up the coffee shop."

"That's right."

"But why weren't we called in for the homicide."

"The other two detectives closed the case, and again not doing a great job. But the FBI are linking him to Travis and his group. Do you know who he is?"

"I did. He's part of ..." Donnie glanced at James.

"Just tell her. I think she's had enough secrecy to last her a lifetime. If this is Daryl Wallace, at least we know what happened to him."

Donnie grunted his approval. "But this doesn't leave the room."

I nodded.

"We're part of a task team to bring down Chicago's underground mafia. Ole Daryl was a runner for them and was sent to give me a message. Even though Daryl wasn't there for you but me instead, it seems as though Travis had him taken care of. Travis must have seen what had happened when Daryl shot up the place, and with you being there, he didn't want Daryl doing it again."

"That makes sense." I turned to the corkboard. "And how is your case going?"

"It's been difficult, but we're almost done," Donnie said, sounding exhausted.

"I can't wait for it to end. This was one of the most diffi-cult cases I've ever worked on."

"Yeah, me too," Donnie said while reading the Post-its on the board. "It looks good. At least now we know who we're dealing with."

"Now we just need to get pictures of our vigilante killers and find out their addresses.

Chapter Twenty-Two

BILLIE STARED SUSPICIOUSLY at the two men behind me.

"They don't bite, Billie," I said and pushed past him. "They're going to help."

"It's just you've never brought anyone around before." He turned to follow me to his command center.

"Desperate times, my friend, desperate times."

Once the four of us were in Billie's basement, I explained what had happened and what we needed.

"He's going to know," was his first response. "The moment I do anything, he will know, and you know this. He's a tricky bastard and needs careful consideration."

"That's why we're here. We need your help." I leaned back in the La-Z-Boy chair and beheld the state of the basement. I knew Billie was a hermit and preferred to stay indoors, but his basement was converted into his bedroom as well. A mattress laid against a wall with the fitted sheet still on, a pillow on top of the mattress, and a duvet folded neatly on the La-Z-Boy beside mine, which James was eyeing. "You can sit." I winked at him. The smell of the place reminded me of a frat house and in desperate need of fresh air. "Is everything all right?" I asked, but Billie didn't answer, he was busy with his PC. "Billie?" I yelled.

"Wah?" He spun around, shell-shocked.

"I asked, is everything okay?" With my right hand, I made a circle in the air, emphasizing the state of his room.

"Oh, yeah, everything is fine."

"Why are you sleeping down here?" It didn't seem like he wanted to elaborate, so I thought I would nudge him.

"I've been hearing noises. This house is so big, and since it's only me in this place while Edwina's in the guest house, I thought I would stay down here and lock the gate." He jerked his chin toward the door where a metal gate had been recently installed with a large lock. He didn't wait for my reply and faced his computer.

I shrugged at James when he shrugged, silently asking me what that was about—I did not know. Billie was careful but not paranoid to this extent.

On our way over, Donnie had made us stop to buy doughnuts, coffee, and sandwiches. I was grateful because I was hungry. We had brought some for Billie too, but he was engrossed with his computer and didn't notice the snacks beside him.

As I watched Billie type, I realized he had lost some weight since I last saw him. His face was thinner, and his clothing hung slightly loose on his large body. Not wanting to make a deal of it in front of Billie, I sent Donnie a text message, letting him know we should keep an eye on Billie. Back when he still worked for the CIA or whichever agency it was, he crashed and burned then too and was hospitalized. I was afraid he was going down that same rabbit hole and didn't want him damaged too badly. And I didn't want Travis to find out about him and come after him.

Donnie gave me thumbs up in response.

James shrugged again, and I showed him the message. After he read it, I deleted it from my phone.

While we waited, we ate what we brought with us and finished our coffee. We roamed around his room while Billie continued as if we weren't even there, and I was sure each of us had memorized every single item in his basement by the time the printer screeched to life. Page after page of information for us to pour over collected in the paper tray, and I couldn't wait to get started.

Billie stood and pulled a stack of printed pages off the tray. "I'm pretty sure he knows we've been digging." His hair was ruffled, and his face was a little paler than before. He hadn't touched the snacks we'd brought him, and his drink was now an ice coffee; we had arrived four hours ago. Billie had barely moved from his desk during all that time. "I did try a few backdoor searches and got what I could, so hopefully this can help you on your mission."

"Thanks, dude," I said and stood while he handed each page to me. "You sure you doing okay? You haven't had anything to eat or drink since we arrived."

"I'm not really hungry. I suppose it's a good thing 'cause I'm trying to lose weight." He laughed, but it sounded forced. "I've planned to take some time off and will be going away for a few days. I'll have my laptop with me, but please don't ask me to do anything. I want to relax, read, play games and little of anything else."

"Oh, yeah sure." I slapped his shoulder and squeezed reassuringly. "It's not a problem. Where are you going?"

"I haven't decided yet, but it needs to be in the sun or on an island somewhere." He handed me the last page.

"Thanks for this. I know we've given you a lot of work

to do these last couple months, and we appreciate it, we really do. I don't know what we'd do without you."

"I just need a break. When I get back, I'll be as right as rain." He walked toward the exit. "Just going to the bathroom then to the kitchen. Anyone want anything?"

"Thanks, but I think we will be going." I lifted the pages in my hands. "We have work to do."

Billie smiled and, with a nod, left the room.

We followed him to the foyer, but where he went to the bathroom, we went toward his front door.

Chapter Twenty-Three

TRAVIS

THE BASTARD DAWDLED into the kitchen like he was already on vacation. "Why the hell did you take so long?" I gripped his neck and squeezed the pressure points. His neck was large, but my hands were stronger.

Billie fell against the tiles, knees first, and stayed still cowering in pain. "I had to make it look legit or she would know."

I considered this; he was right. Dana was a smart woman and would realize if Billie had given her the information quickly—especially since before, he had always struggled. "Okay fine." I released my grip, and he fell onto his hands. Mumbling sounded to my left, and I backhanded the woman again. "And, for god's sake, tell this woman to shut up or I will do more than just gag her."

"Okay, just please leave her alone. She's an innocent in all this. She's the only one who looked after me when my parents were murdered."

"Yes, I saw that." I paced the kitchen. "A home invasion gone wrong but they were unable to find you."

Billie crawled to Edwina and sat on the floor with his back against her legs. It was sweet how he tried to protect her; I almost felt sorry ... almost. Billie nodded, his eyes wide and unsure. Like so many before him, he probably didn't know if I was going to kill them or not. I hadn't made my decision as yet.

"Yes, they almost found me. But Edwina called the cops even though the alarm was going off, and she cared for me once I was out of the closet."

"Ah, how touching," I said, already bored with this conversation. "Did you do what I asked?" I arched an eyebrow.

"Yes. I did everything you asked of me."

"You gave her only the information I gave you?"

"Yes, the information you gave me on the other five."

"And you wasted four fucking hours to do that?"

"She would've known something was up if I was done sooner."

"You're right." I pulled my weapon from behind my back and fired twice.

Chapter Twenty-Four

"ARE you sure you want to go ahead with this?" Donnie asked, testing the earpiece.

We were each fitted with an in-ear earpiece and radio. They were just some of the things Donnie had *borrowed* from the station with Captain Dodd's blessing. Donnie was a star detective and doubted he did anything wrong in Captain Dodd's eyes, so him taking some equipment was absolutely fine.

"Yes, I'm sure," I said, sounding irritated.

We had endured so much during the last four almost five years, and now was the time to strike back, and Donnie was still hesitant. The information Billie had given us brought us to the center—where the group held their weekly sessions. Billie's info had confirmed my suspicions; this was the place where they'd met and had formed their little vigilante group. And they would be here tonight.

"We can forget about this and go home," Donnie confirmed.

"Nope. Let's get this over and done with."

"He just cares for you." James brought me in for an embrace, but our bulletproof vests protected us from each other.

"I know. I just want this over with."

"Me too." He kissed my temple and grabbed the bag.

James followed Donnie across the street, said something to one another, fist bumped, and Donnie disappeared inside the health and wellness center. James crouched behind a trash can while I stood across the street as lookout.

After ten minutes, James's voice crackled in my ear. "Ten-twelve."

I felt the creases between my eyes. James had reviewed the codes with me before we had arrived, and now I'd forgotten what a 10-12 was. "Repeat," I said sheepishly.

"Stand by."

"What?"

"Ten-four," James said and crouched lower.

"Ten-one-oh-one," Donnie said.

"Ten-thirty-one."

"Can't we just talk normally?"

Donnie and James chuckled into my ear, and I rolled my eyes. "You guys are hilarious."

"I love confusing you, sis."

"Not funny," I said, sounding grumpy.

"I see movement up ahead," James said, his tone serious.

Two small lights had turned onto the street and headed in our direction. I saw movement near the service entrance where James was hiding and wanted to tell him to get down; I could still see the top of his head. "Ah, J, get down. I can see your hair."

"They're approaching," James said. "I'm blending in."

I bathed in the shadows and stood behind a tree across

the street from the center. I had sight of both the entrance and the exits while Donnie was inside setting up everything and ensuring nobody else was around.

"Here she comes," I said when I saw a car similar to Aika's.

The red sports car slowed, turned right and entered the parking area.

"And another one," I said.

Instead of either of them responding, all I heard was white noise. I could never get used to these damn things in my ear. I thought Donnie might have grabbed three older models even though the replaceable acoustic tubes were new because they kept switching off and on by themselves —well that's what was happening to mine.

"In coming," James said, followed by the white noise again.

I removed my earpiece and slapped it around. As I replaced it and pressed it against my ear, more vehicles approached, with the black car bringing up the rear. "They're all here," I said and gripped the weapon strapped against my chest.

The vehicles parked, and the occupants exited and climbed the stairs like a group of long-lost friends meeting for a reunion. There was laughter and hugging amongst them. One thing I noticed immediately was they were a tight group. A knot formed in the pit of my stomach, and I wanted to tell the guys to pull back—*It was not a go; I repeat, not a go*—but I was frozen in my spot, and I wasn't stopping them. We were in danger if we continued with this plan, our little mission. We should've asked the FBI to join us but we clumsily agreed not to, it was better if we handled it. We were going after these six highly skilled and extremely dangerous individuals like Girl Scouts selling cookies. They were a group of killers who wouldn't think twice to put a bullet between our eyes. If they knew we were on their territory, they might skin us alive. I managed to open my mouth to tell the two men to pull back, let's rather go home and drink hot chocolate and watch TV. But I closed my dry mouth and swallowed a few times, and that icy feeling slipped down my spine.

Travis was last to ascend the stairs, the leader bringing up the rear. He looked like a regular guy in his jeans and gray jersey, but he was far from regular. He stopped, turned and stared in my direction—at the tree I stood behind. It was as if he had heard my thoughts from here. It was as if he knew I was here, watching them. Travis glanced left and right then continued up the stairs; he was only surveying the area. I exhaled the breath I was holding and shook off my doubts.

"Guys," I said so quietly it sounded more like I was breathing hard instead of speaking.

"What's up?" James asked.

My eyes pricked, but I dared not blink. I swallowed again and cleared my throat. "They're inside." I couldn't say it. I couldn't tell my brother and the man I loved that we had to get out of here, we had to abort our mission. Instead, I stood with a mouth full of teeth.

"Ready," Donnie and James said at the same time.

As much as I wanted to turn around and go home, we couldn't. We had to finish this. Travis would not stop until one of us was dead. I crossed the street and joined James. In a running crouch position, we approached their vehicles.

The information Billie had given us had listed the home addresses for each of them, but, when we drove past each residence, it was clear they no longer lived there. As usual, Travis had no home address listed, but we already had his home address along with his compound where they hunted their victims. Even Aika's home was incorrect on the system, but we already had her real address, and it was under surveillance. The other four were complete unknowns to us, as if they had found a way to live under a different name or with someone else who owned the property and were untraceable.

Billie had given us another piece of information that listed the support group, and they would be here tonight. If we wanted to find out where the others really lived, we needed to follow them from here.

James placed the tracking devices on the yellow Mini Cooper, Aika's red Mustang, and the Silver C-class Merc. I slipped the tracking devices I had on the Dodge truck, the family minivan, and Travis's black Merc. While we were outside doing this, Donnie was inside, recording their group session. I'd told them about what they had said last week, and we hoped they would do the same this week. Donnie planted recording devices under the coffee table and under two chairs. The man who had entered the kitchen while I was trying to leave last week had set it all up for them then left shortly thereafter. I suspected he only came back to clean up after they had left.

Once we had placed all the trackers on each car, we ran around toward the service entrance and entered near the kitchen. We heard voices as we neared the doorjamb leading into the corridor. I stuck my head out and listened. They weren't in the same room they were in last week, and that's where the listening devices were. I turned to mouth the words, *Where are they?* to James who responded by pointing upstairs. It was a good thing Donnie was here and hiding somewhere. I just hoped he realized what they were up to and had followed them to their new venue.

"Where are you, D?" I whispered into my mouthpiece.

Donnie tapped the mouthpiece in response so all we got was a loud *dum dum*. At least he was safe, he just couldn't talk, which meant he was near them.

I glanced at James with wide eyes.

He placed a calm hand on my shoulder and a finger to his mouth so I didn't say anything. He made the hand gesture to move forward. We crept along the passage toward the stairs and passed the bathrooms, the same ones I had used as my exit last week. Instead of going up the first set of stairs, we snuck to the other side and slowly ascended them. The voices grew louder as we approached the larger hallway on the first floor.

From scoping out the center when we had first arrived, I knew this was where patients attended physical therapy. It was a large hall with gym equipment and various medical apparatus.

James pointed to where Donnie had settled—the equipment closet in the corner. "Luckily, I placed bugs there too," he said as we reached him and thumbed the wall beside him. "They haven't said much yet, and it's been thirty minutes already." He pressed the headphone to his ears and shook his head. "It's a dud tonight. They aren't saying anything worthwhile."

I didn't know which happened first, James slamming his body into mine or the wall blasting against our faces. All I remember was flying through the air and James crashing down on me. Debris flew overhead, the door to the equipment room splintered, and Donnie hit the ground hard beside us. I moaned from the impact, my ribs crushed between the floor and James while my ears rang. I nudged James to get off me, but he wasn't moving.

Donnie slowly lifted his head like something heavy was

pressing down on him—it looked painful. When our eyes met, he said something, but I couldn't hear. I saw the panic in his face when he glanced above my head. Donnie reached for his radio while I crawled from under James and found him unconscious and his clothing shredded and bloody. Leaning over him with my cheek against his lips, I felt his breath lightly caress my skin; at least he was still breathing, but he was in bad shape.

I stood to assess the rest of the damage. Debris lay everywhere, and dust particles danced in the air around us. My ears still zinged, and, as I turned, I saw Donnie speaking with someone on his radio, but I still couldn't hear him. To my right was a large gaping hole in the wall from the blast. We needed to ensure the threat was gone before tending to James or any of our wounds.

I pulled my weapon from my vest and approached with caution.

Donnie grabbed my elbow and shook his head and walked ahead of me.

We entered the hall through the new hole in the wall, pointing our weapons left then right, ensuring it was devoid of killers. Smoke floated as we batted the air in front of our faces. In the center of the hall was a table with something on top. We slowly approached the table, ensuring our surroundings were clear. As we neared, we found a tape recorder with the light illuminated green—it was still playing. Although I couldn't hear anything besides the zinging sound deep within my ear, I understood what it meant.

Donnie pulled me out of the hall and pointed at James. He said something and only caught a few words. I think he wanted me to tend to James, which I did.

Kneeling beside James, I saw he was still unconscious.

Donnie was on his radio again, frantically yelling. His

expression changed from anger to sadness to madness in three seconds, only to repeat the process again.

My emotions were all over the place as well. My body was numb yet still vibrated from the blast, like a tuning fork that won't quiet.

Shadows moved on the wall. Donnie and I aimed our weapons, only to lower them the second we saw it was the paramedic running up the stairs. Donnie pointed at James first, then he pointed at me, and I caught the gist of what he was going to do—check the perimeter.

The paramedic asked if I was okay.

I pointed to my ears and said I couldn't hear.

Another paramedic placed a drip into James's hand, applied a neck brace and cut away his vest, followed by his t-shirt. Burn marks and open wounds littered his upper body where the vest had not protected, and I was grateful he had worn it, otherwise he would have been worse.

After a few minutes of watching the paramedic tend to James while the other to me, I heard faint words between the paramedics.

The paramedic covered James and said we were lucky to be alive and that James had most likely suffered a concussion along with the burns.

A cold watery feeling oozed inside my veins, making me shiver. I glanced down and saw the paramedic tape the needle firmly on my hand.

Chapter Twenty-Five

COLD FINGERS TAPPED MY FOREARM, forcing me from my nightmare. I sat upright to find James staring at me. He was lying on his side, an area with the least amount of damage.

"I take it things didn't go down so well?" he asked and sounded like it hurt to speak.

"How are you feeling?" I asked as I stood. I wouldn't allow the paramedic to take James to the hospital unless I was with him.

While Donnie spoke with Captain Dodd about our failed attempt at recording the vigilantes group therapy session, we had arrived at the hospital where a doctor had consulted with me and stitched the cut on my arm from the flying debris that had struck me. James had been triaged then had an MRI done to ensure he suffered no serious head wounds. They had administered stitches on his back and arms and smeared a topical antibiotic cream to his burn wounds to prevent infection.

Dark rings encircled James's eyes, and they sparkled

when he attempted to smile. "Actually, I'm feeling pretty good," he said even though he winced when he tried to move.

I squeezed his hand. "Donnie and I will finish this."

"Give me till tomorrow and I can help you guys."

I climbed onto his bed.

He flinched as he tried to move to give me space, but I told him to stop, and I lay where there was room. We held each other for a moment—a moment I didn't want to ruin, not yet anyway.

A knock sounded on the door and slid open. Donnie entered and smiled when he saw us. "Glad to have you back, buddy."

"I was just telling Dana that I will be ready by tomorrow—"

Donnie shook his head. "No, you're staying here. We're heading out in a couple of minutes." To me, he said, "We have a few blips to check out."

"Why, what's going on?"

"The vigilantes slipped through the back exit before the blast detonated. Dana and I need to see where they are."

"You two can't do this alone."

"We'll be all right." Donnie squeezed my shoulder. "We should go." He jerked his chin toward the door.

I delicately kissed James—even his lip was split—and I climbed off the bed. "See you soon." I squeezed his hand one last time and let go.

Movement caught all our attention, and we faced the door where someone stood with their back to us.

"I have a police guard?" James asked, sounding disgusted.

"Dodd's idea. We need to keep everyone safe," Donnie said and headed for the door. "Get well and see you later."

James mumbled something, but I didn't look over my shoulder or ask him what he'd said. Instead, I followed Donnie out of the room with my head high and my lips closed. I knew if I turned around and said something, James would try change our minds to come with us. But he was injured, and he needed to be safe. I'd seen what his back looked like, and it would take a couple weeks before he could walk without wincing, and he had a drip full of drugs he could self-manage if in too much pain. James hated taking painkillers for fear of becoming addicted but surmised he would be using it a lot this time around.

Donnie spoke in such low tones with the officer stationed outside James's private room that I struggled to hear what they said. He finished, slapped the officer on his back and motioned for me to follow him. As we left the ward, he leaned in and said, "Dodd has been monitoring the group, and one of them has stopped near here."

"What? Really, who?"

"The Asian woman."

"Aika? Her house isn't near here. She lives in Oak Brook."

"Well, her car says she's at a nightclub."

I stopped dead and glared at him with an open mouth. "We can't trust this, Donnie. If we've learned anything, it's they know we're on to them and they already retaliated. We need to be smart about this. We can't just go there."

"You think I don't have a plan?"

"I know you don't have a plan."

Chapter Twenty-Six

THURSDAY

WE HADN'T SLEPT YET, but I wasn't tired when we arrived at the location where Aika was meant to be. For such an early morning, the area was alive with people at one of the more popular clubs. A woman tripped and fell to the ground as she exited the place, with the bouncer closing the door without helping her to her feet. It was a *charming* place so far.

"Are you sure you want to go in there?" Donnie asked again for the sixth time since we'd parked.

We knew we wanted to approach one of them tonight, but the fact it was Aika was pure bliss, and I couldn't wait to turn on the charm with her. "Yes, if you ask me once more—"

"There she is."

Aika exited a dark alley followed by another woman who pulled down her top and buttoned her pants.

"I had no idea," Donnie said, not taking his eyes off either of them.

"Don't get too attached. We might need to kill her."

Donnie made a choking-laughing sound but didn't glance at me.

"And you're sure you still want to go in with me?"

That caught his attention. "What do you think, lil' sis? You know I got you."

"I'm thinking of your family, brother. Just don't get hurt."

We climbed out of his car, crossed the street, and Donnie wrapped his knuckles against the door.

The bouncer opened and stared down at us, his dark gaze filled with suspicion. When he saw we were harmless, he opened the door wider but stopped Donnie to frisk him.

Once we were inside, the heat smacked me in the face while the music pierced my eardrums. Women danced in cages, and one even had an albino Burmese python around her neck and torso. Donnie reached for my hand. I removed his Glock from my waistband and handed it back to him. He tucked it under his shirt and securing it in the back of his pants. I silently prayed he didn't hurt himself.

The dancefloor was packed with people as they moved with the music. We cut through the wave of bodies toward the bar area, the stench of alcohol heavy in the air from years of spillage. The counter was shiny with layers of stickiness, and I avoided touching it, but Donnie leaned on the surface and ordered us beers. I scanned the area with my back to the bar and saw the tall, dark woman dance with her companion in the middle of the dancefloor.

"It looks like it's your turn," Donnie said with a wink.

"She knows who I am, dipshit."

"Just don't tell my wife," he said with a sly grin, grabbed the beers from the bartender and handed me one. He clinked our bottles and left. He stalked Aika and her girlfriend on the dancefloor like they were the only two people around.

My brother had been a dirty flirt before he married and had children, but it seemed as though he still had *the moves*. He danced near the two women and spied them with a predatory gleam in his eyes, and all I could do was roll mine.

I sipped my beer, and the refreshing liquid went down smoothly. My body ached from the blast, and it was just another bruise to add to the bruises already on my body. I would rest when this was over. As I inventoried the people, all I could think about was how James would protest against coming into a place so dark and dingy. In my youth, I used to frequent places such as this one all the time. My friends and I would have a few drinks, dance until the sun came out and then do what we needed to do on only three hours of sleep. But since becoming an FBI analyst and then a PI, I hadn't had time for much of anything or anyone. It was my choice of course, but since James and I started dating, I'd been getting out a bit more—and enjoyed it. From my current surroundings, nothing much had changed; those certain groups of people still existed—those born with a silver spoon rolled up in their dad's cars and spent their money on expensive drinks or on the women they wanted those drinks to be served on. Others sold a new experience to the younger ones, hopefully not killing them in the process but only addicting them to their merchandise. And then there were the clusters of women needing a man to take care of them, and all they could do was show off their *assets*. Lastly, everybody else just wanted to enjoy themselves.

I rolled my eyes again at Donnie grinding against Aika's date who clearly was enjoying the tag-team experience, but Aika was not having any of it. She left the dance floor in a hurry and headed for the bathrooms. Now it was my chance, and I pursued her. Darting through the crowd of hot, sweaty bodies, I made it in time to see her wavy dark hair as she entered the unisex bathrooms. There were about twenty stalls each fitted with a sink so there was no need to converse with the opposite sex while you washed your hands.

As I entered, I saw Aika enter the stall at the end. I headed in that direction and waited outside for her. I sipped my beer and watched others enter, eyed me suspiciously then asked if I needed the bathroom, but I declined by saying I was waiting for my *friend*.

Just as I wanted to give up and knock, Aika's bathroom door opened. Her eyes widened when she saw it was me and not her friend—as if she had thought they had killed us at the center. I suspected she may be a skilled fighter, so I was lucky to have caught her off guard; she didn't see the beer bottle near her face as I smashed it into her and pushed her farther into the stall. Once inside, I locked it behind me and glowered down at her. She cowered and tried to nurse her bleeding cheek. I whipped out my steel telescopic baton from my pocket, now at its full length, and hit her shins. She cried out in pain with one hand on the open wound on her cheek and the other on her shin.

"Did you miss me, Aika?" I asked in a sinister tone I had saved for her. "You asked me all those questions, knowing what you did to me and all those others." I hit her on her thigh, and she cried out again. "How does it feel to be on the receiving end?" I lashed out with the baton across her shoulders and arms, and she flinched each time.

Finally, she stood, her bloodcurdling stare did nothing to stop me.

I hit her across her face and neck in two quick successions because I did not want her to gain strength and come for me. And I was afraid I might back down. What I was doing made me sick to my stomach; I was hurting another person in such a coldhearted way it did not sit well with me. But I needed her to understand I was not someone she could toy with ever again.

Aika sat on the toilet, not knowing which wound to care for first—the cut on her face or the hurt on the rest of her body. It was as if she gave up as she cried into her hands.

My shoulders relaxed, but when she lunged at me, gripping a knife, I instinctively lifted the baton, blocking her from slicing my throat, and kneed her in the groin. She doubled over, leaving her face open, and I kneed her again. Aika's head rocked backward, and the knife flew from her hand as she crashed to the floor between the toilet and the stall wall.

I pointed the baton at her. "Don't make me kill you."

She cackled. Aika was on the ground, at my mercy, and she *cackled*. She had nerves of steel to sit and laugh. I was hoping for a little more bite out of her, but I guessed I'd won this round. "He'll be so mad when he sees what you've done to me." She spit blood and struggled for air.

"What's your involvement?" I needed her to admit what she did within the group.

"He knows everything," she slurred.

I stared down at her, losing patience. I noted one pupil was enlarged while the other small within those haunted blue eyes. I wasn't sure if it was a head injury or if she had taken narcotics.

Her head lulled to one side as she glared up at me. "He knows about your little searches on him and who's been helping you. And he's going to make you hurt so bad."

"What's your involvement?" I needed to hear her say

the words. Surveying the blood-soaked floor and the woman drenched in her own fluids, I realized I could either grab the knife she'd dropped and really hurt her, or I could walk away; I'd done enough damage for now. I picked up her knife, it was heavy in my hands as I pointed it at her.

She watched me carefully with hooded eyes and grimaced. "I like to have a little fun. That's all," she said nonchalantly.

"How many have you killed?" To me, she seemed like the type who liked them weak, afraid, and alone. She was a predator who preyed on those who couldn't defend themselves. And for her to have five others with her to do harm said so much about her character as a person.

"Too many to count," she said, sounding deflated. She gripped her cheek. Blood oozed between her fingers, coating her hand a shiny red. If she didn't seek help soon, she would lose a lot of blood.

"Dana!" Donnie yelled from outside the stalls.

"Yeah?"

"He's here. We've got to go."

"You called him?"

"I saw you and your brother when you entered." She said, her tone disturbingly calm.

As much as I wanted her to suffer, I did not want to go down that same dark path in becoming someone like her. I cleaned her knife and pocketed it. If she bled out, it would be on her terms not mine. "Tell me, who finds them?"

"He does."

"Who is *he*?" I yelled down at her.

"You know—"

"I need to hear you say his name."

"Travis, alright? It's Travis Green. He organizes everything, and we hunt them down at his compound, then we burn their bodies."

"And do you believe they were all guilty?"

She responded with a snort.

"Do you think Travis really cares about you, Aika? Do you think he would risk his life for yours?" I towered over her broken and bruised body. "If you had the option to get out, wouldn't you take it? Save yourself from a death sentence because of one man."

She harrumphed as much as she could without inflicting pain. "Getting out is already a death sentence for us. He would never allow it. He would hunt us down and slaughter us just for thinking about it."

"Help me, Aika. Help me get to him," I whispered. "Once he is gone, you and the others can be free of him."

She shook her head, and her chin trembled.

We wanted Travis, and the only way we could get him was if his group was on our side.

"Come, Dana, we have to leave." Donnie beat against each stall door until I heard him thump against the one we were in.

I opened the door and backed out of the stall but kept my eye on her.

She stayed on the floor, glowering at me.

"Nice job, sis, but we have to bolt."

"Think about it, Aika." I threw a card at her, and it landed on the toilet seat. "You can reach us here if you want to talk." I eased the door closed, and we ran out the bathroom.

The nightclub was still swarming with dancing people as we pushed through the crowd. After a moment of squeezing past sweaty bodies rubbing against us, Donnie leaned near the shell of my ear and said, "He's over by the bar."

I turned in the direction and saw him standing with a menacing gaze, no doubt searching for Aika. Movement caught my eye behind us, and I noticed Aika searching for someone herself.

She found Travis and waved for his attention. When he saw her, she pointed in our direction. He followed her line of sight, but before he could see us, I'd pushed Donnie through the narrow passage and toward the exit.

Donnie bolted out the door with me behind him, and we ran across the street like a couple of kids running from the cops. We climbed into the car, sat low in our seats and waited.

Aika flew out first with Travis behind her. She looked disheveled and bloody, while he was cool and collected as ever. They ran to a dark green Ford, climbed in and drove past us.

Donnie started the engine, turned around and followed.

Chapter Twenty-Seven

TRAVIS

"IT HURTS," Aika cried in the seat beside me.

"I told you not to go out tonight, but you didn't listen. You never listen when I tell you to do something. You deserved this. Do you understand, you deserved *this*. You know, it's a good thing when you called I was nearby."

"Sorry." She pressed one of my gym shirts to her bloody face—at least it was old and could be thrown away. "Do you have anyone nearby who can fix this? My guy is too far away."

I grunted. It was an inconvenience for me to do this, and, as much as I wanted to drop her off on the side of the road and push her into oncoming traffic, she had helped me before, and I owed her. "Yeah, I have someone," I said and headed in the direction of an old friend of mine.

We arrived outside his practice. I helped Aika out the front seat, and she winced each step of the way to his front door. Before I could knock, he opened the door.

"Travis, come, come quickly," the old man said, ushering us inside.

As I entered, I glanced over my shoulder but the streets were empty, and he closed the door behind me.

"What happened?" Gary asked, opening the door to his personal surgery room.

"A misunderstanding," I answered before Aika could. She'd done enough damage; now I had to clean up after her. She was on the verge of tears. I squeezed her shoulder and said, "Lie down. Gary will take care of you."

"Will there be a scar?" she asked quietly, reminding me of a frightened child.

"There will be, but I will do my best to keep you pretty," Gary said as he pulled on latex gloves. Once he was confident his gloves were secure, he reached for his tray of medical equipment. Gary cleaned her cheek wound, injected her with medication and numbing agent and got to work stitching her up.

"I'll be pouring myself a drink."

"You do that, son," Gary said, concentrating on his stitch.

Aika glanced at me, but I wore that expression warning her not to ask.

To Gary, I was the son he never had. I'd visited his practice once about fifteen years ago and been seeing him whenever I needed to. Occasionally, I would stop by for a drink and bring him a few bottles of whiskey. Now that he'd retired from surgery, he spent his days with his birds and long walks to the park with his little mix-breed dog, Dash.

I could hear Aika's whimpering all the way to his kitchen. It served her right; she should have gone home when I told her to. She knew of the possibility that we would be watched, but she didn't want to listen. I returned to the surgery room, and Aika was stitched up already. "That was quick."

"There's more stitches inside her mouth. Luckily, it wasn't that big a cut, but it will hurt for a while. She has bruising on her shins, head, and back which should clear in a week or two. And I would lay off any narcotics for a while." He eyed her suspiciously.

"Good. Thanks, Gary. I'll see you in a few days."

"Alright," he said as he cleaned his medical tray, removed his gloves and washed his hands.

I helped Aika off the surgical bed.

She winced but walked in a crouching stance. Dana had worked her over pretty well, which made me proud but at the same time angry because Aika knew better.

We left Gary in his surgical room and exited his front door, closing it behind us. The streets were still quiet and dark by the time we reached my car. I opened the door for Aika. She climbed in and sank her body into the seat, a sigh escaping her lips as she relaxed.

The ride to her house in Oak Brook was an icy silence. She kept stealing glances my way, waiting for the bomb to drop.

I kept her in suspense until I parked near her house and left the car idling. "Get some rest. I'll need you this weekend."

"What's happening this weekend?" she asked nervously.

"It doesn't matter, just be ready." I revved the engine. "Now get out, I want to go."

Her expression forced me to say what I was actually thinking. "Don't give me that look, Aika. You knew the risks, especially when I told you not to go out. And what did you do? You went out. We just blew up a wall to scare Dana and her lover. We are wanted criminals. Do you understand? They are after us"

Tears welled in her glacier-colored eyes, but she didn't answer me—she knew better.

"How can you think you had the freedom to go party? What's wrong with you? And next time, don't call me when you have a suspicion someone might be on to you. Or I will kill you myself. Now get out and away from my car."

She glared daggers at me and wiped her face as she climbed out. She slammed the door so hard the car rocked.

I would have to teach her a lesson the weekend.

And to think she had been my *favorite*.

Chapter Twenty-Eight

FRIDAY

AFTER WE SPOKE with the retired doctor who knew nothing about Travis's extra curricula, Donnie and I had crashed at the hospital in James's private room. There was no safer place to get a good night's sleep than here with a police guard outside the room, not forgetting the two stationed at the entrance and one at the exit of the hospital. Donnie had pushed together two chairs and slept with his feet on one and his knees against the wall while his head lay on a pillow on the backrest and against the wall. I had climbed onto the bed with James, and it felt like I died for a few hours I slept so heavily. When I awoke, my neck hurt, but at least I was with James. Careful not to disturb him, I climbed off his bed. The coffee was like sludge, but it would have to do. As I reached the door to slide it open, Captain Dodd marched down the corridor.

"Are they awake?" he yelled, making the nurse at the station flinch in surprise.

"They are now," I mumbled to myself and kicked Donnie's feet.

He shot upright and stood in attack mode, wiping sleep from his eyes. "I hate it when you do that."

I swallowed my laugh when Captain Dodd entered.

"I don't know what you did, Donnie, but she made contact." He slapped Donnie's back.

"I doubt it was me, Captain, but thanks for the compliment. Dana here did most of the heavy lifting," Donnie said with a wink.

Captain Dodd barely registered I was beside them. "Aika called the number on the card you gave her and wants to spill the beans for protection. The FBI will arrange for a meeting this afternoon. With her confession, we finally have enough evidence on Travis. We need to secure this witness after she's signed her statement."

"And if he kills her before she can do that?" I asked.

Captain Dodd peered down at me, waiting for me to add to my comment.

"Travis's program is linked to the various institutions and will know what we are up to, especially if this is entered into the system. Aika will show up dead, by accident of course, and we are back where we started. We can't allow him to find out."

"The FBI are aware and are taking special precautions."

"I hope so, for everybody's sake and especially Aika's."

"Walk with me, Donnie. This may be your chance to work with the FBI." Captain Dodd laid a hand on the back of Donnie's neck, and they exited the room.

James stirred.

I approached his bed and climbed on to lay beside him. "I don't trust anything that comes from that group. First, they try to blow us up, and now this. It has to be another trap."

"Or Aika realized who she was up against and wants to get out."

"I doubt it." As much as I wanted to believe that, I didn't. These killers were ruthless, and I didn't think they had it in them to come forward. The last four years that group had been silent, yet people were still going missing. Whether or not they were responsible was yet to be seen. With no evidence or witnesses, Chicago Police couldn't do anything. Nobody had any idea where the group of vigilante killers even were until recently. And, if Aika really wanted to come forward to tell her side of the story, I would be surprised. Perhaps I needed to see for myself whether she was serious or not.

———

I DROVE to the house where I knew Aika lived and surprisingly saw her red Mustang in her driveway. I knew she hadn't been home since last Friday but it would seem she was back—perhaps she knew her house was being monitored and felt safer. I parked behind her car, traversed the path to her door and knocked.

"That was quick," she said as she opened the door, but her smile disappeared when she saw it was me and tried to close the door again.

I'd stuck my foot between the door and the frame and winced from the impact. "I don't want to hurt you, Aika. I just want to ask you questions." I backed up slowly and lifted my hands.

She didn't slam the door in my face. I heard her swallow, and it sounded like it hurt.

"Your face looks good," I said and meant it. I didn't

think she would have a horrible scar and felt relief I hadn't disfigured her.

Her eyes flitted to the scar on my cheek and gave me her deadpan glare. She exhaled a shaky breath, glanced at our surroundings and opened her door wider. "Come in but be quick. Damian is on his way over."

"I shouldn't be long." I stepped into her foyer but stayed near the open door. "Are you seriously coming in this afternoon to give a statement?"

"Yes." She nodded with misty eyes. "I just want this over. I can't carry on like this." She dabbed a tissue over her eyes and leaned against the wall. "I'm not a monster. I know the difference between right and wrong. In the beginning, I thought it was right what we were doing, but ... but it's getting worse. He is getting worse and dangerous." She checked her watch. "You have to go. Damian should be here, and he will hurt you if he catches you here."

I had to wonder whether Travis had threatened her, and, in my opinion, that could've been a reason for her to approach us. It was only a matter of time before he would turn on the people he'd relied on for so long. What they were doing couldn't last.

"Okay, thanks." I turned to exit her house. "I might be there when you come in. Maybe we can talk afterward." I glanced at the wounds on her face and smiled sincerely.

"That would be nice, thank you."

I ran to my car and sped away. I didn't want to be here when Damian arrived, but I did want to see what he was up to. I drove around the block and edged slowly back to her house. I'd left just in time. As I neared her house again, I saw his Dodge truck parked behind her car.

They spoke for a few minutes by her open front door,

then he returned to his truck and left. Aika waved and turned to go inside.

Damian stopped at a pharmacy and came out with a package. He drove to Aika's house and walked to her front door with the package. He gave her the package, kissed her and traversed back to his truck.

I sent Donnie a text asking him whether they were still tracking the vehicles, and he replied by calling. "Why are you asking?"

"I just wanted to know."

"You never just ask anything. Dodd said they have all their locations and have one person monitoring them. I just followed up with him earlier, and he says they are all at their homes except one of them."

At least they hadn't discovered the trackers. "Thanks."

"What are you doing?" he asked suspiciously.

"Damian is at Aika's house, dropping off medication."

"The redhead?"

"Yeah," I said and placed my phone in the handsfree kit.

"He's probably the one who isn't at home."

"Yep." I tapped the gas pedal, and the car inched forward. "I have an idea." Everything may have changed, and I wanted to know if it was just Aika who felt that way. "I have to go. He's on the move."

"Dammit." He sighed but resigned to the idea. "Okay, but only follow him, Dana. Be careful and let me know where you are. I need to tie up a few loose ends this side and can meet you somewhere."

"I promise," I said and ended the call.

The haunting look in Aika's eyes was real, she was scared. She had said Travis was worsening. It was good news that Aika was coming in to give us her statement. We might need more than just her on our side. Travis could discover what she had planned and kill her, then we would have nothing. We needed at least one or two others to join her, provide statements, and offer any other useful information on Travis we didn't already know—what they had done with the bodies of those they hunted and killed would be a great start. The more of them on our side, the better chance we had of getting Travis. Based on Damian's and Aika's interaction with each other, I suspected they may be close. I recalled Damian's case; a drunk driver had killed his wife when the car struck her. It was his *kill* that fateful night four years ago when I stood face to mask with them. As fearful as I felt, I needed to approach Damian and use his relationship with Aika to get through to him—they could be a happy couple somewhere away from Travis. Although I doubted they would be free, the justice system would be after them no matter what they told us. If he joined Aika and they both gave independent statements, it could assist our case. And perhaps he could convince one of the others to join. But I first needed to see if he would willingly do so.

Damian drove within the speed limit and stopped at a hardware store.

I parked across the street and approached the store. Once inside, I took a left and checked the aisles to find him. I walked farther into the aisle and grabbed a screwdriver then put it back down.

Damian held a different sized hammer in each hand, inspecting the grip, weight, and how they felt when he brought each down.

"Can I help with something?" I asked and approached.

Damian nodded. "Yes, please." He turned and froze when he saw me. His mouth hung open as if trying to formulate words, but all he could do was stare with wide eyes. After a moment, he glanced down the aisle on both sides and lowered his hands and the hammers he gripped. "What are you doing here?"

"What do you plan on doing with those, Damian?" His expression changed when I said his name, like he didn't expect me to know it. But then his demeanor shifted, and I couldn't quite read him.

He shook his head once as if dispelling a bad thought. "You shouldn't be here," he said, his tone dark and deep.

My arms pebbled. It was crazy for me to approach him in the open like this, but I thought it was safer than at his home. At least here I could cry for help, but I doubted he would try anything anyway. "I needed to speak to you without any of the others around."

"It's dangerous to speak to me here." He spied the cameras, and a cold feeling engulfed me when I glanced up.

"Is he watching?"

"If he's watching you, maybe." He gripped the hammers tighter, making the leather creak.

I stepped backward and gripped the boxcutter in my hand behind my back. "He has access to camera feeds?"

Damian turned his glacier-colored eyes at me and stepped backward. "You are going to get me killed. He's been obsessed with you since that night. For you to come here and speak with me might send him the wrong message."

"Are you afraid of him?" I stepped closer to Damian.

Sweat peppered his forehead as he kept eyeing the cameras and down the aisle, as if he suspected Travis would magically appear. "Aren't you? After everything he's done to you, you have the balls to come here?"

"Help me get Travis, Damian. Help us with information. We can hide you and Aika. He won't be able to find either of you.

That caught his attention, and, at first, he seemed confused, then he relaxed a little. "So, it's true? You seriously want us to come in, give our statements and, just like that, he will disappear. Aika mentioned you left a card for her to call you or the cops or whatever, but I didn't believe it. And I will tell you what I told Aika, that she's dumb to go to the cops, because Travis will know. He knows everything." Damian swallowed; I watched his Adam's apple bob up and down. He wiped the sweat off his brow and checked over his shoulder. He sucked in air and checked the aisles again. "You do understand there's no way for anybody to get Travis. He's paranoid enough not to get caught. The man is untouchable. He has information on everybody, and, if anyone tries to go after him, he uses that info on them. It's impossible."

"Who said anything about arresting him?"

Chapter Twenty-Nine

I FIRST THOUGHT Damian wanted to rip off my head with my suggestion, and I was ready to fight him in the hardware store, but then he agreed, however only if Neal joined them. The more we had on our side, the better chance we had to defeat Travis. I gathered from his choice of words he too was afraid of Travis and would feel comfortable if more of them were on our side, which was a relief. Damian would be the one to assist with the persuasion and recruitment, but he wanted me to tag along.

I followed Damian to Neal's house, a double-story mini mansion with a yellow hummer parked outside. The information Billie had gathered for us didn't stipulate their income or what it was each did for a living, but based on that monstrous gas guzzler and home, Neal did pretty all right for himself. But what surprised me more was this wasn't the residence we had tracked him to. I messaged Donnie, letting him know where I was and to send someone to check the place where his *other* car was parked. He had no doubt been covering his tracks and had a decoy residence where he just parked his car and climbed into his other one to come to his real home. He was smart, but I could only imagine the constant level of anxiety he had to be in, always looking over his shoulder.

"You brought her to my house?" Neal asked through gritted teeth. "I worked so hard at hiding my address, yet here you come, bringing the enemy right to my doorstep." He stomped toward his garage. "What's wrong with you, Damian? Is this a trap? Did she bring cops with her?"

"Calm down, Neal. It's just us. And we're all on the same side."

Neal harrumphed and walked around the side of his house toward a building near his pool.

We entered behind him into an office.

"She'll get us killed. You know what he'll do to us when he finds out we're speaking to *her*." He pointed a finger at me.

Again, they sounded as if they too were afraid of Travis, and I wondered what he had on them.

"What will he do to you?" I asked as I closed the door. I couldn't explain it, but I didn't feel afraid for my life—not like I had when I was in Travis's company. The two men seemed just as afraid. They kept glancing around as if someone lurked in the shadows. I noted Neal had no cameras anywhere on his property, most likely by choice.

"Ah, you don't want to know, little girl. You don't want to mess with Travis." Neal approached his desk and moved a photo frame so I couldn't see it.

Damian told Neal the reason for my contacting them and what I wanted to do.

Neal listened to him, but he kept shaking his head.

"Are you with us?"

"It won't work, Damian. I mean, I hear you, loud and

clear, but that man ..." He left his word hanging in the air. "I know he threatened Aika, and I know what she means to you, but we can't go against him." He glared at me as he spoke.

"You'd allow him to kill Aika? I know Dafne would be on our side. The two of them haven't ever gotten on. And, if we had to toss a coin on who got to kill him, she would fight us for it. She would be happy to put a bullet between his eyes."

Neal sighed, fell into his office chair and swiveled it to face the window, not answering Damian.

"You know what we've been through with this guy. There's no other way. You know what he's done to us—"

"Don't say it!" Neal yelled. "Just don't say it."

"Maybe you need to hear it again, because we have a way to get out." Damian thumbed in my direction. "If we all do this together, we have a chance."

"I want papers. If everyone agrees to do this, we are exonerated from our actions."

I shook my head. "That won't happen, I'm sorry. What you all did was awful. You killed people, slaughtered them like animals and burned their bodies. The very least you will avoid the death penalty."

"If we stay, it's a death sentence. If we go along with this and he finds out, it's a death sentence. Either way, we're screwed."

"Did you know that Travis conditioned us?" Damian asked me.

I shook my head, not understanding what he meant.

"Don't, man—"

"You need to hear this again, Neal," Damian said then faced me. "Travis used his program to *find* us." A low sarcastic chuckle sounded from Neal, but Damian ignored him. "He built his little team of designer killers by using his Doe program. By using various keywords to penetrate various systems to get our medical records, he found a handful of people who may be predisposed to violence—and he used that against us. For two years, we sat with him in our little support group as he egged us on and convinced us how revenge was the only way we could cope with our loss. For six years, we have been in his toxic environment that drove Dafne crazy and suicidal. If you ask me, Travis did something to her—"

"Don't!"

Damian pointed at Neal and shook his head. "I know it's hard for you, but it's hard for all of us to know Travis created a killing team based on lies." He refocused on me. "At first, it was fun. We thought those who had wronged us were guilty, but they weren't. It was the version of the truth Travis wanted us to hear. Dafne's husband had a girlfriend and wanted to run away. Aika's husband was scum and was robbed and stabbed. Joe's brother was more upset being compared to Joe than he was of his friends. The man who hit my wife wasn't even drunk. It was what Travis told us to believe, and we believed him."

"My sister was a druggie, and we ignored that," Neal said with heartfelt emotion. "And he likes to threaten Dafne. She's easy pickings. She used to like him—as in, wanted to date him—and he messes with her because of it."

"She told me he choked her last month. He enticed her to come over, then when she did, he choked her and kicked her out. Or rather, he hit her, and she fell," Damian said.

"All the more reason for all of you to band together and help me stop him."

Neal turned to me. "When last did you see your friend? It was so easy for Travis to find him, give you information he wanted you to have and then kill him—and his house manager. It's easy for him to find us and slaughter us one by one if he ever found out we were talking about this. You have no idea what you are dealing with."

I swallowed hard. Neal was referring to Billie. We had just seen him a couple of days ago. Now that I thought about it, he had been acting a little strange—more stressed than usual. He had told us he was going away for a while, and because I'd been so busy thinking of ways to get Travis, I hadn't concentrated on my friend's behavior. And the information Billie had given us had led us to the health and medical center where they met weekly—ready for an explosion. I pulled my cellphone from my pocket and dialed his number—it went to voicemail.

"Sorry, Dana, but your friend is dead," Neal said.

"You almost sound happy about it, Neal," I said through gritted teeth. Exhaling a shaky breath, I couldn't allow myself to get lost in the sadness. I needed to push through, or everything would've been for nothing. When I found my voice, I said, "If he's dead, I can't do anything about it now, but we can still do this together."

"How do you propose we do that?"

"You make him think you've captured me."

"That's crazy. You want us to take you directly to him?"

I nodded. "Right now, his defenses are up, waiting for us to strike next. I would rather be taken to him and let him think he's won. With your help, I'm sure we can subdue him before he knows what hit him."

"You're nuts." Neal shook his head and turned toward the window again. "He'll see right through it."

"Maybe, but we will still have the upper hand. And I will have you guys to help me."

"I still want assurance that we won't get the death

penalty and they will suspend our sentence to a maximum of six years with parole," Neal said as he stood.

Damian stared at his friend as if it was the first time Neal had taken a stand for anything.

"Fine. I can't promise everything, but I will see what I can do." I sent Donnie a text message. I was sure he could get the FBI to agree to their terms. If they wanted all of them to cooperate and not just Aika, this was what they had to agree to. And it was a way for everyone to walk out of here alive. It had to be done.

Chapter Thirty

"I DON'T LIKE THIS." James pressed his lips to my temple. "Let the FBI handle it."

"You know I can't. If he has so much of an inkling they might be involved, he will kill all of them."

He sighed like the world was pressing down on his chest, but I was lying beside him with my head on his shoulder. "Heaven knows they deserve what comes their way. But what I can't believe is the FBI agreeing to their demands."

"It was an agreement, not demands. They will all serve jail time for their involvement."

"But not long enough."

"It's the best we can do. We need to get Travis, and this is the only way. From speaking with Neal and Damian, Travis isn't too happy with his group, and they're all scared he might go after them. Then, when he's done with them, I'm next, possibly even you. He knows everyone I love, and Donnie might be next, his kids, even my parents. I can't let any of that happen. And for any of this to work, we need them. You and I know it."

He sighed like he had more to say but couldn't. He held his breath and kept quiet. I didn't know what that was all about nor did I want to press him—whatever it was, we could discuss it when I returned.

"Well, at least you love me." He teased, trying to make light of the subject.

I slapped his shoulder gently, I didn't want to hurt him. "You know I do." I purred, raised my head and kissed him.

"I can't wait until you show me." He caressed my back then over the curve of my hip and kissed me again. "What time are you leaving?" He squeezed me closer to him.

"Around seven." I checked the wall clock—we had an hour left. "How are you feeling? When I got in, I didn't even ask you." I leaned on one elbow to face him.

"Better. I can lie on my back without wanting to curl in the fetal position and die." He pulled me into an embrace again, and I wrapped my left arm around him.

"As much as I love lying here, I need to grab some food before I go. I'll need my strength. Who knows what'll happen or how Travis will handle this?"

"What will happen? You and them are heading to his compound, and then what?"

"Let him think I've been captured."

Chapter Thirty-One

TRAVIS

I WATCHED Aika and Damian hug goodbye, then Damian climbed into his truck and drove away. She blew a kiss as he left, and I knew I had to finish this before he came back. I couldn't do this if he was near. Once I was confident he wouldn't return, I parked in her driveway.

I whistled as I traversed the path to her front door. In my head, the silent melodies I heard in tune with each footstep, the beat of drums, and delicate keys of the piano was soothing and made me smile.

It was the calm before the storm.

Those sounds were only for me, and although some had said it's not right that I heard them, I knew I was special because of it. I'd stopped seeing the doctors and the shrinks because they couldn't help me, and I threw away their pointless medication. There was nothing for them to fix.

I felt happy about what I was about to do; it was passed its due date. I'd had my fun with the group, but that nagging feeling was still there, telling me to *watch out, be careful, they see through you*. That I needed to close the loop or something awful was about to happen.

One would assume I would go for Dafne first; she was my first choice after all—that history repeated itself and, boy, did we have an awful start. But after the way Aika had glared at me when I had dropped her off was a warning—a punch to the gut. She was my prized pupil, yet her mistrusting gaze held enough forewarning that now was the time, and she needed to be first—the catalyst to my impending doom.

Not only had the authorities seized my company's documents and searched my house, but the FBI was on to me, actively seeking me out. They wanted to bring me in for a page full of charges, which I knew I couldn't get out of—not anymore. And Dana was in on it. Just when I thought we were doing so well, that we were growing closer as a couple, she had to stab me in the back. Then there's Aika. She gave me that look of disappointment that could not be ignored. She was the weak link in our group, and I had to do something about it—about her.

Using the set of keys I had made, I unlocked her security gate then knocked on Aika's front door.

"Did you forget something?" she asked, but her face dropped when she opened the door and saw it was me and not Damian. "Travis, what are you doing here?" She closed the door ever so slightly, hinting that she did not want me inside, and she did not open the security door.

I flung open the security door and hit Aika in the face before she could retaliate.

She fell backward into the wall, jumped to her feet and ran to the end of the hallway as I entered her foyer. Her bedroom door snapped shut followed by a lock turning.

"What have you been saying about me, Aika? What

have you been telling them?" I roared, slamming her front door shut. I stalked toward her bedroom. I'd been here enough times to know each and every room and what they held—her room did not have secret passageways or a window big enough for her to climb out of. "I know you've been speaking about me. I can feel them, Aika. I can feel them after me. I can sense what you and the others are trying to do. I just don't know when." I banged on her door. "What have you been saying!"

"You're crazy, Travis! You've completely lost your mind." I heard the distinct clicking sounds as she readied her weapons.

I knew the quality of the doors and kicked at her bedroom door. My foot went straight through the soft wood. I pulled out my foot, crouched and peeped through the new hole I'd made. I saw her sitting on her bed, her face as white as a sheet, as she fumbled with her gun. Her cellphone was laying on her bed and the screen was on. "I see you," I growled in a low voice I knew would scare her, taunting her as I had others so many times before at my compound. She always hated when I did that. Choosing to stand away from me during our hunts, she thought I didn't know—but I did.

I jimmied the lock with the screwdriver I kept in my car and forced open the door. She raised her weapon in my direction. I lunged for her and slapped the gun to the floor. Aika was a tough woman and a fighter; she had moves that could make men blush, but she was injured and not as quick as she usually was. Her face was swollen and most likely tender. Her appearance screamed pain.

I elbowed her in the face.

She cried out but not before hitting me in the groin.

I crashed to the floor. The sting of pain shot down my

leg and up my spine. She turned to flee, but I grabbed her foot.

She tripped and fell, knocking her head against the hard surface. I lunged at her again, but she kicked me away and hit me in the chest, knocking the wind from me.

I brought out the screwdriver from the side and struck her temple, driving it into her head.

Her arms went limp, and her eyes rolled into the back of her head. Blood pumped from the wound when I yanked out the screwdriver. She flopped to the floor as she expelled her final breath.

Standing up, I cast an eye to her room and to her phone. I saw the name on the screen. She'd called Dana, and she was still on the call. I pressed the end button and wiped my prints from anything inside Aika's house, closed the door and drove away.

Chapter Thirty-Two

I STOOD outside Aika's house with Damian. He'd called me after he'd returned from buying an early dinner for Aika and found her lifeless body. I was still at the hospital with James when she'd called me but had left a voice message. I only heard her message—of her fighting Travis and then her death—after I had arrived at her house and spoke with Damian. He had asked me not to call the cops, but I had to bring Donnie with me—it was either that or the FBI.

"He knows," Damian said, nervously scanning the street and the houses next door.

That was my thought too, that somehow Travis had found out we were conspiring against him, that I had infiltrated his group of vigilante killers and turned them against him. But what I couldn't understand was if Damian or Neal had mentioned it to him, why? It would only put their lives in danger. There had to be another reason. Somehow, someone had told Travis what we were planning, like he was always one step ahead of us.

"If he does know, who told him and why? Only you and Neal know about the plan, unless you told someone else."

"I didn't do it, and Neal certainly wouldn't have. He knows what would happen if he said anything. We all know what Travis is like and what he would do to us if he found out we want to turn him into the cops."

"It had to have been Aika," I added.

"She was scared of him, especially after this last incident. She would never tell him," Damian said as he chewed on his bottom lip. He had this habit where he rubbed his shirt between his index finger and thumb, and I wanted to grab his hand to stop him but didn't. "I left to buy her an early dinner before she went in to give her statement. I was only gone for, like, an hour. When I returned with her food, I found her like this. I suspect Travis waited for me to leave before going into her house."

"I'm sorry, I really am."

"Now what are we going to do?"

"I don't know—"

"We continue with the plan," Donnie interrupted. "Captain Dodd thinks the same and has pulled in additional resources. Nothing is logged into the system, so there's no way he would know what we're up to. You and the others meet Travis tomorrow like you usually do. It is on Saturdays when you all hunt someone?" It sounded more like a jab than a statement.

"Yes ..." Damian continued to rub the end of his shirt. "Last time didn't go so well."

"What happened?"

"Let's just say Dafne *really* hates him." He sighed. "But we may have another problem."

"What's that?"

"He hasn't told us to meet him. He always tells us when

and where. We don't just arrive at his place. And since his compound is compromised, he must find another spot. Only if he has, then he might call."

"Okay, we can work with this. Phone him and say the cops killed Aika and ask if it's still happening tomorrow," Donnie said.

Damian considered this for a moment. "That could work. If he thinks the cops did this" —he pointed at Aika's house— "he *might* be convinced."

"Great. Then tomorrow it is."

"Just remember he's unstable," Damian said nervously.

"Do you have anything else you want to share with us, Damian?" Donnie asked, suspiciously scrutinizing Damian.

"He records each hunt, then, when it's over, he makes us watch it with him. He pours us each a drink, and we watch it with him. He even laughs sometimes. Although, the last time ended with him collecting his camera and storming off. He has a collection of recordings. Maybe if we get those instead of trying to lure him out …"

"The recordings will help the case, but we still have to lure him out, Damian. At the moment, we don't know where he is," I said as I nodded at Donnie.

"Then why don't we first wait until we have him in custody or wait until he's dead."

"He might destroy this evidence before then. Where does he keep them?"

"Since his compound is out of the question, he no doubt moved his hard drive to his other apartment."

"Jeez, how many properties does he have?"

"A lot! He's a creative accountant."

Chapter Thirty-Three

THE OTHER APARTMENT Damian had mentioned was the building next to the one where I had been held hostage—the one with a *For Sale* sign. It made me wonder exactly what Travis was up to with an empty building, even though it was for sale. It reminded me of a Venus flytrap, waiting for an insect to crawl inside—and I was the insect. I didn't like this and voiced my concern.

Donnie rolled his eyes and entered with Damian close behind. "It's just a building, Dana."

"He left the building unlocked, Donnie. That alone should make your skin crawl."

"It will be okay." Donnie smiled, trying to reassure me, but it didn't help.

"From what I understand, this is the only building he doesn't have cameras. But"—Damian eyed the corners of the foyer—"that could've changed since last month."

"Isn't he afraid someone might squat and never leave?"

"If anyone enters and decides not to leave, Travis will

turn it into a sport and hunt them here," Damian said it in such a way that it had already happened before.

"We need those tapes."

We followed Damian through the foyer and into the stairwell. We entered the fifth-floor corridor and stopped outside a door with no number. If I was here on my own, I would have completely missed the door, as it looked like it was part of the wall. The only discerning element that this was a door was the razor-thin space between the door and the wall.

"You must be kidding me," Donnie said as he knocked on the wall, informing us it was solid. When he knocked on the door, it was very hollow.

Damian pressed one side of the door, and it sprung open. "I was the only one Travis ever brought here." He entered the dark room and fumbled for the light switch.

Once it was on, I saw the room was barely big enough for the three of us to stand in. I pushed past Donnie toward the desk with screens. "Was this a supply closet or something?"

"Probably. Travis told me his father had owned this building. When the market changed and people lost their jobs, some occupants moved out, while others were evicted. I don't know why he wants to sell it, it's downtown and near all amenities. But, knowing Travis, he does things without logic." Damian shrugged and searched the drawers of the desk. "Got them," he said and handed Donnie the hard drive.

"Let's get out of here." Donnie turned to open the door but froze. "Where's the handle?"

Damian pushed against the door like he had for us to enter, and it clicked open.

As we exited, the elevator sounded, and the doors opened.

"Is that him?" I whispered to no one in particular.

"I seriously doubt anyone else would come here, and definitely not this side." Damian pointed at the door he just closed.

The way to the elevator and stairs was to our right, with nothing to our left except for a window.

Donnie pulled the handle, and it easily slid up. "Let's get out of here," he said and climbed out.

I heard his boots step on the tiles then the hallway carpet as he headed this way.

I climbed through the window and stood on the ledge beside Donnie and waited for Damian to join us. "Hurry," I said as I shuffled on the tight ledge with my back flat against the wall. I did not want to look down. The wind had increased, and, if I dared to move, I was afraid I would fall the five stories to the ground below. Luckily, the window looked across the back where the refuse was collected and not the street where we would be seen.

Damian climbed out and closed the window. He pressed against the wall beside me just as we heard the door click open and close shut again.

I exhaled a shaky breath and clung to the wall.

"Let's go back inside." Donnie nudged my arm beside his.

"Are you crazy? He's right there."

"I know, but we can't stay out here, and there's nowhere else for us to go but down. I suggest we go inside before he finishes what he came to do and catches us."

Damian didn't need an invitation. He opened the window and climbed inside.

The warmth was a comfort as I gripped the windowsill.

Damian was already heading for the door to the room where Travis was when I had a leg inside. The door opened. My heart thumped, and I stood like a statue.

Damian ran quietly around the corner and out of sight as Travis exited his room and clicked the door shut.

I stared at him, praying he didn't turn around and see me. I retracted my leg into the cold again. I didn't want to close the window in case it made a noise, because, for the life of me, I couldn't remember whether it made a sound. I pressed my back against the wall and squeezed my eyes tight. I heard his footsteps on the carpet as if he were right beside me. I heard him breathe and hoped I was hearing things. I opened one eye and turned to my left. The window was open, but I couldn't see him. I nudged closer to Donnie who gripped my arm. The window slammed shut. My heart stopped for a second, and I held my breath. The worst was hearing him lock the latch at the top.

"Oh, my gods, we're stuck here," I whispered near Donnie's ear. "He locked the window."

"Give it a second. Hopefully Damian comes back," Donnie said unconvincingly.

I realized I had to look down. If Damian didn't return, we needed another way out of this mess. Gripping hold of Donnie's arm and the wall, I glanced down then quickly looked up again. I had to stop being afraid of heights and tried again. An empty garbage container stood directly below us, five stories down. "There's no way we can climb down—"

I flinched at the sound of the window opening and Damian sticking out his head. "The coast is clear." He grinned and disappeared.

Chapter Thirty-Four

DAFNE RAN in front of the camera. Blood covered her back and the right side of her face. She jumped on top of the man trying to crawl away. The man seemed disorientated as he struggled to focus, and I doubted he was aware of his surroundings following the beating he'd received. Dafne lifted her hand holding the hunting knife and hesitated.

"Do it!" the voice behind the camera commanded. Travis spoke in a low, deep growl that made my arms pebble every time he told Dafne what to do. "Now!"

Dafne whimpered and brought down the knife, killing her victim.

"I don't want to see anymore." I moaned from my seat. We'd seen six similar snuff films that we had to pause halfway through to take a breather. In each video, Travis had instructed them what they had to do. Or rather, he barked his orders or threatened them with life or limb. "Please switch this off." I stood and headed for the door.

Donnie paused the video with the image of Dafne now

standing and facing the camera frozen on the screen. Blood covered her face as tears streaked her cheeks. "I think I've seen enough as well." He turned to Will, the now-paled FBI agent who had joined us, and handed him the television remote. "Knock yourself out."

"I think we have more than enough evidence for the death penalty." Will placed the remote on the table beside him. "And you say everything is arranged for tomorrow?"

Damian nodded. "After we left the building, Travis called. We're to meet at Wolf Road Woods tomorrow at nine. He says he has someone special."

I'd recognized that area.

"That's where Nails's body was dumped, wasn't it?" Will asked.

Damian nodded.

"Did he see you there?"

Damian glanced at me then Donnie. "I didn't see him when we left."

"What if he was hiding and saw you exit, and this is a set up?"

"We are prepared for that," Donnie said and pushed me out the door.

"What?" I asked when we were down the passage heading toward the break room.

"Just in case one of the knuckleheads logged anything, I've brought in Marc who is ready to extract you from the chaos."

"Okay."

"You have to listen to him, Dana. I'm not joking. We don't know what Travis has planned, and someone has to get you out safely when all hell breaks loose—"

"I got it."

"As discussed with the FBI and Captain Dodd, we will

get there a couple hours before the scheduled time, and you will ride with Damian. And, here." He handed me one of their newer tactical vests. "It's one of the smallest, so it should fit."

"Thanks." I took the vest from him. "Are you coming with me to the hospital?"

"No. I need to finalize a few things with everybody for tomorrow. You sure you know what to do?"

I rolled my eyes—"I'm a hostage, I don't have to do anything"—and grinned.

"Smartass."

———

IT WAS late by the time I entered James's private room. The policeman sitting outside his door tipped his head in greeting and continued reading his book. The nurse's station was empty, but I heard low murmurs from one of the rooms in the corner.

James was asleep when I stood beside his bed. The cut on his forehead wasn't as swollen as it was before, and his cheeks were multicolored green and purple. I'd suffered a few cuts that required stitching, but he had protected me from the main blast, proving once again how much he loved and cared for me.

All I wanted more than anything was for us to do things like a normal couple without having to look over our shoulders for a maniac who had an itch he needed to scratch.

I carefully took his hand in mine, and he stirred, his eyes fluttering open as he wiped his face with his free hand.

"What time is it?" He squinted at the wall clock.

"A little after eleven. How are you feeling?" I sat beside him and rested his hand in my lap.

"Better. I don't need painkillers every three hours."

"That's good." I gently pecked his cheek. "I thought I would sleep here. Have an early rise tomorrow morning."

"Are you seriously going along with it?"

"Uh-huh. Everything is arranged and should be fine."

The expression James wore said enough; he didn't need to say he was worried, and he hated the idea.

I knew and understood. I curled beside him and nestled my head on his shoulder.

He winced from the movement but didn't tell me to get off.

"I know you don't like the idea, but it will be over soon." I entwined my fingers with his. "Then we can get our lives back. Go hiking, camping, sleeping under the stars—"

"And skinny dipping!" He squeezed me closer to him.

"Oh, definitely." I smiled at the delicious memories and couldn't wait to make more.

Chapter Thirty-Five

SATURDAY

I ARRIVED outside Damian's house, paid the taxi and climbed out. We'd agreed to meet at Damian's house because it was closer to Wolf Road Woods than any of the others. He'd said Dafne was thrilled to learn of the plan and had asked for the kill shot. I agreed to this. My understanding was Travis had treated her worse than he had me. He taunted her psychologically, while he had only caused me physical harm. Actually, he'd taunted us equally but in different ways—we'd both have our way with him. Donnie was the only one privy to the real plan; the FBI and Captain Dodd were under the impression they were arresting him.

I saw the family van parked beside Damian's Ram and knew Neal was here. The family minivan Neal used was his decoy vehicle and had parked it by a house he didn't live in. Across the road stood a Mini Cooper which I presumed belonged to Joe, and the silver Mercedes was Dafne's.

A strange feeling developed inside the pit of my stomach that I didn't like. It felt like a million insects were crawling inside as the hairs at the back of my neck stood on end. Damian didn't say anything about speaking with Joe. From what they'd said about Joe, Damian didn't think he would go for it. They thought he was too close to Travis and did everything Travis told him to do. They were worried Joe might not want to betray Travis and would reveal our plan. But, if his Mini was here, they must've persuaded him—I hoped.

"Hello?" I called into the house and pushed open the door wider. The foyer was warm even though the front door had been standing ajar. The smell of coffee wafted in the air, and I relaxed my shoulders.

"We're in the kitchen," someone replied.

I passed the living area where magazines lay on the floor, and the fireplace was on. A roaring fire heated the area, and I suspected that was the reason for the warmth. I continued toward the kitchen. I'd followed Damian to his house yesterday, so I knew where to come to this morning. And, as suspected, the other residence where he had left his vehicle was another decoy residence—this address was where he slept. But he liked his Dodge Rams; he had one similar to the decoy.

Low murmurs emanated from the kitchen. When I entered, all heads turned and stared at me. I noticed their wide eyes first. Secondly, I noticed tape over their mouths except for Joe's and Neal's. Red rope bound Dafne to the chair, and Damian had a knife through his hand and pinned to the table. Tears streaked both their faces, but Damian had received a beating. His eyes were swollen shut, and he had a cut above his right eye. Blood everywhere.

I had less than a second to react. I was outnumbered without backup. My backup was already at the rendezvous. In that slow second, I reached for my weapon and fired at

Neal. I didn't know which of the two men were better fighters or marksmen, but I hit the one closest to me.

When Neal went down, Joe reached for his weapon and fired at me.

I jumped backward and collided with a warm body. Remembering what had happened the last time I had walked into someone, instinctively I fell to the floor before Travis could chloroform me.

He reached for me as I fell to the side, raised my weapon and fired. I hit his chest, but he didn't go down. Travis dropped the cloth in his hand and ran into the kitchen.

Taking deep breaths, I stayed on ground level and peered around the doorjamb. The kitchen door was open, Travis was out, and Joe entered my line of sight. He aimed at me, but I managed to take a shot before he could. The bullet struck his shoulder. He crouched and darted out the back door.

I checked behind me and entered the rooms off the corridor. They were void of other attackers, but the thought of someone lingering nearby still made me feel uneasy. James's words repeated in me, and I felt very stupid. I'd come to Damian's house alone, thinking everything would be fine, but it was not fine. It *was* a trap. I was the insect and about to get eaten.

I retrieved my cell and texted Donnie. The Woods weren't that far from here, but five minutes driving while trying to stay alive would feel like forever. I cursed myself again for coming here alone. Stupid. Stupid. Stupid. But I couldn't do anything about it now, except fight back.

I slowly entered the kitchen, still crouching, and peered around the doorjamb. Wide eyes blinked at me. The back door stood open. Beneath the table, I saw two pairs of legs and one dead Neal. Blood oozed from the headshot, and dead eyes stared through me. I shuddered but was grateful my hospital breakfast didn't repeat on me.

"Are you injured?" I yelled as I stood and tactically approached Damian first. I unsheathed my knife and cut him and Dafne free. They removed the tape from their mouths. I grabbed the hilt and said, "Count to three. One..." I yanked the knife out of Damian's hand and the table. Damian screamed in pain and nursed his wound. Once he'd settled down he and Dafne spoke at the same time. Dafne gave up and allowed Damian to speak.

"I tried to get rid of Joe, but he wouldn't budge. He usually stops by my house before our hunts, and when he arrived and Dafne was already here, he knew something was up. I tried to get him away, but it didn't work. Then when Neal arrived"—he eyed the body near his feet— "he rambled on about how it wasn't his idea. They subdued us and waited for you."

"It's okay, but we have to go after them. Where could they have gone? I didn't hear a car start."

"There's a path that leads directly to the woods," Damian said, hesitating.

"What?"

"They knew, Dana. They knew you were coming and that you would be alone. They didn't have to call Travis. He was already on his way over."

"Do you think someone tipped him off? Nobody logged anything in case Travis was monitoring."

Damian nodded, and his expression said it all. Someone was giving him information—either the FBI or from Donnie's station.

"Who do you think it is?"

"I don't know. Travis didn't always tell us everything. He

would arrive and say we needed to do this, that, or the other. We knew his program gave him a lot of information, but someone close to you has been leaking information. Travis knew about Billie, knew where you lived or had moved to even though it was on a family member's name. Travis even told us what you liked to wear to bed." Damian swallowed hard, and I joined him.

I clenched my teeth so hard my jaw ached, and when the back of my throat stopped aching, I finally said, "Did Travis ever install cameras into my home?"

"Your first apartment, yes, but none of your other places. He could never get a key to gain entry, so he always relied on the information."

I was very careful what I said to whom. Only my brother and parents knew where I lived. Marc and Nigel knew of my previous homes before I'd met James, but they didn't know about the new place I'd moved to. And the only person who knew what I wore to bed was James.

Oh, my gods. No. No. No.

As much as I didn't want to believe it, perhaps I had to come to terms that maybe, just maybe, it was James. They had attacked me at my home after Donnie had told James where I'd stayed. Donnie had told James at one of our family Sunday lunches. Then I had given a statement to James. And from then, James had started pursuing me. When the pig heart had arrived, I had stayed at James for a few days.

I bit my lip until I tasted blood as I considered the turn of events. Ever since James had come into my life, Travis's attacks had escalated. When James had been shot, only Donnie and Marc had known we were hiking. Had James been injured on purpose so I didn't suspect him? When I had been drugged from drinking the wine and Travis had carved the pig into my cheek, it had been convenient that I was alone. My arms pebbled at the thought that James was working with Travis.

The person James had always been fighting with on those phone calls could've been Travis, had Travis wanted him to hurt me there and then. It reminded me of the types of questions Travis had asked during our *sessions*—How is your new boyfriend? Travis had asked with the demeanor of a psychologist. I'd told him all about James and how happy we were. And, for once in my adult life, I was truly happy, that James had given me the confidence to do everything with him.

I pulled my cellphone from my pocket and dialed James's cell—no answer. I dialed the nurse's station at the hospital. When they answered, I asked if James was there.

"No, dear. He checked out about thirty minutes ago. He said he was feeling much better and would be going home."

"Thank you." I ended the call and felt blood drain from my face as my skin prickled with deadly anticipation. Was James coming to help Travis kill me?

"Where did he go?" Dafne asked. She'd been very quiet the entire time until now. She rubbed the welts on her wrists.

"They say he went home, but he isn't answering his phone." As much as I wanted to fall into a corner and cry, I couldn't. They were on the run and needed to be stopped.

"Well, what are you waiting for?" Damian asked as he grabbed his compound bow from his pantry cupboard. "Let's hunt the bastards." He grinned.

Chapter Thirty-Six

TRAVIS

WE'D EXITED Damian's house and ran the path that led us to the woods. It would be the best hunting ground for us, and our prey would be glorious. My cell rang. After glancing at the caller ID, I answered. "Where are you? We're about to start."

"I'm coming. Just make sure she's still alive by the time I get there."

"Don't worry. We'll all take turns hunting her. We can maim her and set her loose each time. With you, me, and Joe left, we should have a lot of fun."

"Good. I've been waiting so long to do this. Finally, we have prey worthy of our talents."

"You're a sick bastard—"

"Not as sick as you." He chuckled.

"Be careful. The charges are about to detonate." I ended the call and ran to catch up with Joe.

"Everything in place?" he asked, grinning.

"Yep." I pulled the detonator out of my pocket and hit the red button.

Chapter Thirty-Seven

DAFNE GRABBED the Glock from the kitchen counter and headed for the back door while Damian went into one of his rooms. He returned to the kitchen with a tactical vest and grenades.

"Who are you planning on blowing up?"

"He won't fight fair, Dana. This is the only language he knows."

"Good to know. Let's get out of there."

We exited through the kitchen and approached Dafne already at the far end of Damian's property wearing a bored expression. Her arms were crossed, and she leaned to one side. "Where were you guys? One moment, we were heading out; the next, I was on my own."

"Enough with the bitching, Dafne. I had to get my toys," Damian said as we reached her.

Behind me, a whirr sounded, as if an engine had started, followed by three clicks. Damian spun around, most likely hearing the same thing, and grabbed me. He pulled me to the ground while Dafne followed suit. A moment later, heat and bright light flashed above us, followed by debris flying around us. Shards of glass rained down while the back door flew past, splintering into a million pieces upon contact with the wall.

Glancing over my shoulder, I saw Damian's house had been blasted into a ball of hateful flames and angry fire. If we had taken a moment too long to get our stuff and get out, we would've been blown up into chunks of flesh. They would have to scrape what was left of us off the ground.

Damian groaned beside me. Splintered wood and shards of glass had struck one side of his face, making him look like a pincushion, and guilt struck me—that could've been me five seconds ago.

"Thank you."

"I have a lot to atone for." He groaned.

"Will you be okay?" I asked, knowing it was a stupid question but still asked anyway.

He rolled onto his back and chuckled painfully. "Yep, but it'll be a bitch." He sat upright and surveyed his surroundings. "He blew up my house." He grunted. "Now I have to blow him up," he said sadistically, making me scoot farther away from him.

Dafne moaned as she sat upright, but she was okay; I couldn't see any injuries. "I really hate him. If only I could go back five years and start over."

"Yeah, but unfortunately, we're stuck in this timeline," Damian said.

"Did you tell her how he coerced us into doing what he wanted?"

"Yep."

"Does she know that none of our first victims were really guilty?"

"I think I did mention something along those lines when we were at Neal's house."

"I want to tell her my version. If I'm killed today, at least I said what I needed to say." Dafne turned her striking-blue eyes at me. "None of our initial victims were truly guilty. He had brainwashed us over the years into thinking they were, but they weren't. The night of each kill, we would ask our victim to repent. And every single one of them gave another story of what really happened. At first, I thought they were talking bullshit, but I did some of my own digging. William had been under the drinking limit, and it was Damian's wife who had hit his car, not the other way around. She had skipped the traffic light and plowed into him. Neal's sister was a drug user and overdosed. She was home alone and had bought from her drug dealer. The two boys Joe had accused of bullying Jacob were friends and just as insecure. But it was Joe who Jacob had been trying to measure up against. I read the suicide note, and Jacob had mentioned Joe's name and how their parents always favored him—"

"When did you find out?" Damian asked.

"It was only recently when I started digging. I wanted to make sure that if something happened to me, the truth came out. Aika's husband had lost their money but not the way she'd first thought. He was the one who had started the pyramid scheme, and he was the one swindling money from unsuspecting clients. If you ask me, he got what he deserved."

"What about you?" I asked.

"That night we were in Jack's home, he had told me my husband wanted to divorce me and travel with his lover. I hired a private investigator to do some of my own digging and found it was all true. And the best part was, it was his

girlfriend who had broken into the office and killed him."
She cackled. "How ironic! What a bastard."

"Because he already knew your stories," I said. "He had
you believe the others were guilty. He twisted the events
slightly yet still believable."

Damian and Dafne nodded. "He's a conniving asshole.
And he knew just how to play us all. And somehow, he had
managed to keep his hooks in Joe and Neal so deep there
would be no out for them," Damian said.

"This ends today," I said.

Dafne stood and pointed her weapon at the path. "Shall
we do this?"

Chapter Thirty-Eight

WE FOLLOWED the path into the woods. It was a vast area where families used to come for picnics, but after the murders, they avoided it, with good cause. Now it was a hunting field for Travis and his killers. As we traversed through the dense vegetation, Damian told me everything. I'd switched on my recorder as proof in case something happened to us. The voice recording would automatically upload to the cloud, and I had already sent Donnie and Marc my passcodes in my untimely death.

I'd phoned Donnie and had told him what had happened, and we were on our way. He replied there was a mix up with the venue, and only two men had arrived with him. He had no idea what had happened, but something was wrong. And Marc was stuck on the side of the road somewhere with a flat tire. I told him my thoughts about someone leaking information and who I thought it was. He didn't believe me, naturally, and had called me back when he tried to reach James. Apparently, he too couldn't get hold of him. He apologized again for what had happened to me, but it wasn't his fault. I'd fallen for a man I thought loved me but was in a partnership with an evil and sadistic killer. Which meant James was just as evil and sadistic for leading me on and playing a game of cat and mouse with me. I did not appreciate the events, but I was glad my brother was still alive and was my backup.

After a brisk thirty-minute walk, we stalked into the woods. Travis, Joe, and James could be hiding in plain sight, and we had to be careful. I smelled smoke and wet leaves. Doubting someone could make a fire with anything from the woods, I chalked it up to the explosion and that the wind had most likely blown the smoke this way. Apart from the smell burning my nostrils, nothing besides creatures and little animals moved through the woods. I glanced at the treetops in case any one of them were hiding high and had a bird's eye view of us—we were easy targets.

"Let's split up," Dafne said as she moved left.

"That's the worst idea ever," I said. "We need to stick together, that way we can fight together."

Sighing, Dafne came back in behind us. "Fine, but I'm killing the bastard."

"Don't worry, I'm sure we will have our hands full."

A loud crack sounded, piercing the silent air. I glanced around, and the movement of something behind me caught my eye.

Dafne's head rocked backward. Her eye exploded as brain fragments was blown out the back of her head. She crashed to the ground with a thud as Damian raised his compound bow and released the fiber-tip arrow. It whooshed through the air as it flew past me.

I turned to see its target, and it struck Joe in the chest and pinned him to a tree.

Joe raised his weapon, but I fired my Glock before he

had a chance. The bullet struck his neck, and he died a slow death as he gasped for air and dropped his gun.

Birds flew overhead from the gunshots, and footsteps neared. Damian and I stood back to back as we surveyed the wooded area for any more attacks. If someone had told me last week I would be teaming up with a known vigilante killer, I would've laughed in their face. Yet here I was, working with Damian, and, as strange as it sounded, I was grateful he was a skilled marksman.

The running didn't stop until I heard leaves crunch underfoot.

"Don't move!" Damian yelled.

I glanced over my shoulder and Damian's to see who had approached us.

"Are you okay, Dana?" James asked.

I raised my gun at him and scanned for more threat. "Why are you out of the hospital, James?"

"Something felt off. I had to see if you were okay."

"Why didn't you answer your phone? Donnie and I have been trying to call you."

"My phone is dead."

"That's a little too convenient, James." I kept my weapon trained on him. "Was it fun working with the enemy?"

"What?"

"You heard me. But, in case you're hard of hearing, I will repeat myself. Were we ever real? Or was going after me the thrill of it? How long have you and Travis been planning this?"

Confusion crossed his features. "What are you talking about? I'm not—"

"Stop right there." Another voice sounded behind us.

I spun around to see Captain Dodd and his weapon

aimed at me. It was a Mexican standoff where everyone was guilty and all pointed a gun at someone. My gun was on Dodd, his on James, James pointed at Damian, and Damian pointed at James.

Movement caught my eye, and Travis entered my line of sight. His knife was pointed at me, but he was the only one close enough to do me harm. I shifted my attention to him instead and aimed for his head.

"What the hell is going on here?"

I didn't have to turn to see who had spoken, Donnie was here. "I need a little help, Donnie. I don't know what's happening here. As far as I'm concerned, shoot James and Travis."

"What? Why me? I'm here to help you," James said, sounding wounded that I wanted him dead.

"Where were you, partner?"

"I just told Dana I thought something didn't sit right, and I came here to help. It seems I was right."

"Why didn't you answer your phone?"

"It's dead—"

A gun fired, and a body crashed to the ground.

"That's enough," Captain Dodd said as he lowered his weapon. "This wasn't what I wanted, but I guess I'll have to improvise," he said amusingly and crossed the tall grass to stand beside Travis. "Now, now. Put that down, or I'll kill your brother."

"You?" I yelled, panning between Dodd and Travis. I heard Donnie come closer as he murmured something.

"Stand where you are, Donnie, or I'll really enjoy gutting her," Dodd said, waving a hunting knife that eerily resembled Travis's.

"What happened to you, Captain? Why?" Donnie asked, sounding just as shocked as I felt.

He shrugged. The highly intelligent captain shrugged. Of all things, it's as if he had nothing intelligent to say. "I love the thrill of it, the chase. I've never felt so alive before in my life." He smiled sinisterly.

"I met your captain after my parents died, and he left quite an impression on me. When I was a little older, I contacted him to ask him to train me. I attended the best classes money could buy, and since then, we've remained close. He helped secure my contracts with the various agencies when I was ready with Doe. I confided in him what I wanted to do, to *really* do, and he said he wanted in. We went *hunting* on a regular basis like any father and son would. Unfortunately, he couldn't hunt with my Horsemen for obvious reasons. But I always saved some of the best for us."

"You're both sick," Damian said behind me. I could feel his anger radiate off his chest as he aimed his arrow at Dodd. "You are a police captain. You are meant to protect the public and your officers. You just killed one of your own and who knows how many others."

I now realized the body that had fallen was James, and my heart constricted. I'd just accused the man I loved of working with a serial killer when it wasn't him. I wished I could go back in time and change my final words to him. But it was too late.

I opened my mouth to add to what Damian had said, but warm liquid splashed my face, making me flinch. Dodd was the kind of man who was a few steps ahead, keeping an eye on his environment while conversing at the same time. But he didn't see James sit upright and fire his weapon at his captain. The bullet hit Dodd in the face, and he fell hard to the ground.

When I wiped his blood from my face, I glanced to the

side to see James kneeling on one leg with his arm trained at his former captain. I wanted to run to James and shower him with love, but a blur of something rushed past me.

Donnie knocked Travis to the ground. Travis's concentration had been on his killing buddy, and he didn't see Donnie crash into him. Donnie groaned in pain and gripped his side.

I pulled the trigger and hit Travis in the shoulder.

Damian fired another arrow. A *thwish* of the string sounded as he released it, and the point struck Travis in the chest, missing Donnie by an inch.

"You almost hit my brother." I slapped Damian's chest and ran to the two men on the ground.

James approached behind me, pulled off his vest and spoke into his radio.

Donnie crawled away from Travis, clutching the knife in his stomach, and Travis tried to sit upright. He didn't get far, because James kicked him in the chest, sending him to the ground where he pinned him to the spot.

"You have to kill me. Or I'll just keep coming after you, her, and *you*." Travis scowled at Damian behind me.

"Oh no, you aren't." I didn't hesitate. I'd had enough. I fired consecutively until one side of his head was a mess.

"That's enough. You're empty." James grabbed the Glock out my hands and pulled me into an embrace. He kissed my temple and whispered near the shell of my ear, "I love you. I would never hurt you. I'm sorry I couldn't tell you everything."

That caught my attention, and I pulled away from him and frowned.

"I was investigating Dodd. That's why I came here. That's why I was assigned to your brother. You had nothing to do with it, I promise. It was just a wonderful coincidence." He smiled and tucked loose strands behind my ear.

"You knew about Dodd?" I asked, feeling more confused than before.

"I knew he was dirty. We knew he was part of some hunting sport. We didn't know he was part of Travis's crew."

"Did you know he would be here?"

"When you told me what was happening, I checked in with my real boss. He said there was strange activity on the system which Travis and Dodd used to communicate. They penetrated the firewall, got hold of the transcript and notified me. If they were a minute too late, this would've ended very differently."

"I can't believe it." I wrapped my arms around his waist. "Why didn't you just arrest Dodd? Why take so long?"

"I was still collecting evidence on him. Remember all those heated arguments I'd had over the phone?"

I nodded.

"It was about this, about Dodd. My direct report wanted results, but I couldn't go after him before I knew for sure he was involved with Travis. Then when all this happened, I knew it was time to strike."

I felt guilty for doubting him, for thinking it was he who had joined forces with Travis. I hugged him closer.

"I can't believe you thought it was me," he said as if reading my thoughts. "How on earth could you think I was ever involved?" He chuckled lightheartedly and kissed the top of my head.

"In that moment it all pointed to you. I wouldn't have thought Dodd was involved in a million years. I still can't believe it. I'm just glad everything worked out in the end."

"Me too," he said as the wailing sounds of sirens cut through the air. "Donnie, are you okay?"

Donnie nodded. "Yeah, it's a flesh wound."

"Then why are you still on the ground?"

"I didn't want to interrupt your moment with my sister."

James reached out, and Donnie grabbed his hand, both men wincing as James helped Donnie up.

Once Donnie stood, he removed his vest and lifted his shirt to reveal a cut on his side that bled worse than it was. "See? Flesh wound."

A paramedic ran toward us. He saw the bodies on the ground and looked unsure where to go to first, but we all pointed at Donnie, making his decision easy. Damian was fine, as was I, and James had worn his vest. The shot from Dodd's gun had hit his chest and would only leave a bruise. We had all gotten away easy compared to how it had all started.

I really thought I was going to die today. But I was glad it was over and that James was not the bad guy I had thought he was. Even though I had thought it for a short while, I still felt guilty and skeptical at the same time. I'm sure with time it will all go away.

Chapter Thirty-Nine

SUNDAY

SITTING around the table with my family was the best thing I'd needed. We'd all escaped death yesterday, and I squeezed James's hand that held my knee. The man who had been tormenting me for over four—almost five—years was dead, along with his accomplices.

Damian had pled guilty to murder but due to his good behavior and cooperation would only serve about five years. The FBI had closed their case, as did Donnie.

My dad handed me the salad bowl, and I added some to my plate and passed it to James. We said a prayer, my dad thankful none of us were badly injured and that he had all his kids around the table and his grand babies. My mom wiped away tears with her napkin, and we proceeded to eat.

My body was bruised and sore, and even my heel was aching from the thorn that had to be removed. It would take a couple of days or a week before I would feel *normal* again. But it was a small price to pay, and I would accept this discomfort any day.

James kept his hand on my knee, and I kept my hand on

his. He didn't mind eating with his left hand and every so often would squeeze my knee—constantly showing he cared and loved me.

I loved him too.

Marc and I would continue with the business, although he had said he was ready to retire. He wanted to visit his daughter for a couple weeks in Europe and would decide whether he would sell the company or hand it to me— whichever I preferred. It was a big responsibility that I would consider.

James had confessed to being part of internal affairs and had asked to permanently transfer to Donnie's precinct and to keep his current job. Donnie said he would consider it— then two minutes later, he'd shaken James's hand and welcomed him to the precinct.

We agreed I would move in with him and possibly adopt a dog. Neither of us were ready for children yet, although anything was possible.

We were happy, things would be normal, and we could finally live our lives.

Steve Campbell Psychological Suspense Thriller Series

vinci-books.com/campbell1

Unraveling evil, one missing girl at a time.

In the small town of Ketchum, Detective Steve Campbell is faced with a chilling case: two women have gone missing, abducted a month apart.

Turn the page for a free preview

The Last Girl: Chapter One

THE CABIN

Jacob
1987

The quiet evening pierced my ears. Carefully, I climbed out of the water and onto the wooden deck without making a sound. I exhaled silently as I monitored the couple fast asleep in the boat. Tiptoeing on the wooden deck, I was careful not to stand on a creaking plank and when I reached the door, Katie stirred in the boat, mumbling someone's name. I opened the door, testing to ensure it didn't moan the wider I opened it, and slipped out.

I traversed the dark path to the house and entered. Leaving the lights off, I navigated my way around the living room, kitchen, until finally upstairs. I entered the main bedroom and found his suitcase again. Flipping through his wallet, I found what I was looking for and headed back down to the kitchen. Their food remained on the counter, waiting for them to enjoy, and I opened the pantry door.

Once done, I slipped out the front door and found a

place hidden in shadows where I could see most of the house and waited. I heard cars driving on the ID-75 entering and exiting Ketchum and was grateful they were a distance away and wouldn't see me or my vehicle from the road.

It was ten at night by the time Katie and her friend staggered up the path, switching on lights as they entered the house and headed for the kitchen. Katie warmed their dinner while her friend sat at the table, waiting for her to serve him.

The itch at the back of my neck started up again, but I didn't scratch. I just rubbed the offending area and waited.

Katie dished food onto their plates and sat beside him. My body heated as I watched him eat. All was fine for a few seconds and then… he grabbed his throat. His eyes widened in horror. Red blotches formed on his face and neck. His face started swelling, along with one side of his neck. He pushed away from the table, stood up, then doubled over as if trying to expel whatever was lodged in his throat.

Katie was there to slap him on his back, but nothing helped.

Nothing would help him.

The man pointed to the stairs and then to his neck. Katie nodded and frantically ran upstairs.

Moments later, she returned, shaking her head. "There's nothing there," she cried.

Shock flashed in his eyes. He collapsed onto his knees, then fell on his chest and face, unmoving.

Katie dashed around, looking for something, but there was nothing that could help him. She fell to her knees and moved him onto his back so she could proceed with CPR, but his throat had already closed, shutting off all his air supply.

From where I stood, his face and neck had swollen to the point where his cheeks were red, round and puffy, and his eyes had bulged. While his fat lips had started turning purple.

After about ten minutes, Katie sat back on her haunches, crying into her hands.

I dropped the epinephrine injection on the ground and crushed it with my boot heel. Pushing through the branches, I approached the cabin with purpose and entered through the front door.

Katie flinched when she saw me and stood up. "Jacob, what are you doing here?" she asked, glancing nervously at me and then at her friend on the floor.

"I thought you might need some help," I said mysteriously and crossed the threshold. My clothing was still damp, and I left wet marks everywhere I stepped.

Katie backed up, glancing at me and the body. "We need to call for help," she stammered, "could you—"

"No," I yelled, shutting her up. "No more, Katie," I snapped. "You've been playing me for years. No more." I pulled the box out of my pocket and placed it gently on the counter. "I've had this for a while, waiting for the right moment to give it to you. To ask for your hand in marriage. Ever since that day in the barn, I've loved you more than anything else. I would've given you the world, anything, and everything you ever wanted. But," I paused for effect and stared into her sad, blue eyes, "you've made it perfectly clear where I stand with you."

The Last Girl: Chapter Two

Michelle
2001

Jessica combed her long blond hair and tied it in a low ponytail. She fixed her black top; the one I had bought her for her birthday with the famous Rolling Stones tongue. Then she fastened her belt and pulled on her coat. Grabbing her makeup bag, she applied eyeshadow, mascara that made her green eyes brighter, and lipstick sparingly, transforming her youthful face into a more mature look.

We had become best friends since first grade in the Ernest Hemingway School in Ketchum. Since then, we did nothing without the other. Once a month, we visited Mike, our good friend, and went to O'Brian's Pub for a few beers and a couple of games.

"How do I look?" she asked, twirling.

"Like you're twenty-two," I said, grinning. I pulled on my coat and huddled into it. "How about me?"

"Perfect," she said.

I wiped some makeup out of the corner of my eye and smiled. My eyes had thick eyeliner, highlighting my big brown eyes, and I tied my black hair in a low ponytail. I had a fair complexion and with my hair being naturally black; I looked like a porcelain doll. But I was not as beautiful as Jessica.

"Are you two wenches finished?" Mike yelled outside the bathroom. "I'm hungry, and there's a game with my name on."

"Yeah, yeah, we're done," I said, opening the door.

Mike stood in the doorjamb, blocking my way. He wore his signature black outfit; black army boots, black cargo pants, and a long sleeve black vest with a black jacket over. With his brown hair shaved close to his head, he reminded me of someone who should be in the army and not out drinking.

I waved the air in front of my nose. "You smell like weed again."

"I know. You want some?"

"No, thanks."

"Come," Jessica said, pushing past Mike, "there are men who need to buy us drinks."

"You're such a skank," Mike said, chuckling, his smile reaching his light brown eyes. If it wasn't for the gothic clothing he wore, I thought he was handsome.

"You're just jealous you can't get free drinks." She cooed.

"Whatever, now come," Mike said, jogging down the stairs. "Bye mom," he yelled into the lounge. His mom waved and continued watching her fantasy series.

We climbed into Mike's blue van, his Passion Wagon, and drove the short distance to O'Brian's Pub. It was a quaint little drinking hole where a lot of the residents frequented. The place smelled like stale ale. The bar counter was sticky from years of spillage, and the beer flowed all night long.

Mike parked the van in the only available parking spot, which was right at the back underneath the one lamppost that didn't work. We traversed the recently cleared path as snow continued falling around us.

I entered the pub first, and the heat smacked me in the face. Shivering from the sudden change in temperature, I headed for the bar and stood between two men talking about their workday.

"Oh, I'm sorry. Am I bothering you?" I asked, fluttering my eyelashes.

"No, sweetheart," the man on my right said. "But I would love to buy you a drink?"

"A beer will do," I said, smiling sweetly.

"Hey Nancy," said the same man, "get my lady friend here a beer."

"Make that two, please, kind sir," Jessica said behind me.

"Make it two," he said with a wicked grin. "And who might you be?"

"Jessica," she said, holding out her hand for him to shake.

Nancy gave us our beers.

The man stood to retrieve his wallet from his back pocket, paid, and sat down again. Jessica and I stood on either side of him and kissed him on the cheek.

"Thank you," we said together and disappeared into the crowd near the back, where Mike was already playing a game of pool.

We laughed and joked around. We tampered with

Mike's cue stick every time he tried to take a shot, sipped from his friends' drinks, and enjoyed our evening.

I loved coming here, as did Jessica. We were together, we always had fun, and we never had to pay for anything.

"I feel like a shot," Jessica said, swaying slightly.

"You've had enough," I said, slipping my arm through hers. "How about we ask Nancy for something to eat and two glasses of water?"

"Nah, I want a shot." Jessica unhooked her arm from mine and made a beeline toward the bar. She bumped into a man wearing a blue jacket sitting at the bar and started talking to him. She laughed at whatever he said and sat beside him. They seemed to enjoy each other's company and now and then, Jessica would touch his arm or laugh at whatever he said. Then she thumbed over her shoulder at me. But the man didn't turn around.

Mike cut in front of me, blocking my view. "Move," I moaned and pushed past him. When I could see Jessica again, she downed a shot with the man and then he stood up from his stool. He pointed at the door, and Jessica nodded.

"What are you doing?" I mumbled to myself.

"Where are you going?" Mike asked.

"To stop Jessica from making a big mistake."

"She's a big girl. She can take care of herself."

"She's only nineteen, Mike," I grumbled. "We need to look out for each other."

Mike raised his hands in mock surrender. "Fine, but if you aren't here when I'm ready to go, I'll leave your ass here, too."

I rolled my eyes and headed for the door. Jessica and the man had already left by the time I pulled on my coat. I opened the door, and the cold air stole my breath as I braved the chilly night.

A car's engine rumbled to life in the distance, and I turned to look, but couldn't see much. A light came on and I squinted.

"Jessica?" I yelled and headed for the car. "Jessica?" I yelled again, waving my arms so she could see me.

A car door slammed, and a figure headed my way. "Michelle," Jessica said, closing the gap. "I'm going home with my new friend." She wiggled her eyebrows. "I'll see you at Mike's tomorrow," she slurred, hugging me. When she let me go, her now dull green eyes glazed over as she smiled.

"Are you sure you're in condition to go home with anyone?" I asked.

"Relax, I'm fine. Besides, everyone knows him," she said, turning around.

"Who is he?" I asked. There were moments like now when I hated going out with Jessica. She had gone home with guys once or twice before, but I had always met them beforehand. I didn't know who this guy was, and it left me worried.

"It's fine, he's fine, I'm fine," she mumbled. "I'll see you in the morning." She waved over her shoulder as she walked to his car.

"Who is he?" I yelled, but she didn't hear me.

Once Jessica climbed into his car, he turned around, blinding me with his headlights. Once I could see again, all I saw were his taillights in the distance.

I didn't like her going off with some stranger she had only just met and even though he was someone everybody knew, apparently; I didn't know who he was.

Something didn't sit right with me, but I shook off the bad feeling. She was a young adult and could handle herself.

When I went back inside the pub, I had sobered up and asked Mike if we could leave. He handed me the keys and asked me to drive.

Once back at his place, I settled into the bed beside him, and he started snoring; I laid awake with worry.

———

The next morning, when Jessica didn't come home, I asked Mike to take me to the police station. I waited to speak with an officer, filled out forms, and explained what had happened.

When Monday came and went and Jessica still hadn't come home, and I hadn't heard from the detective, I went back to the police station. They reassured me they were investigating and would give me feedback by Wednesday.

Wednesday passed, and the detective called me on Thursday to let me know they had no leads or witnesses. He also informed me that there were many people at O'Brian's Pub and Nancy didn't remember Jessica or me being there, therefore nobody knew who the man was she had gone home with.

When Friday arrived and I still had heard nothing, I asked Mike to go with me to the pub, but because Christmas was next Tuesday, he was taking his mother to visit his aunt in Sun Valley.

I went alone to the pub, but it was empty, with only a few patrons; none of them remembered me and I couldn't recall them either. I came home early and vowed to go the next weekend and the next until I found out who Jessica's kidnapper was.

If he was local, he had to return.

The Last Girl: Chapter Two

TOUGHEN UP

Jacob - 8 years old
1974

Mama had a headache and didn't join us at church today. Papa told me we had to hurry home because he needed to tend to the sheep.

"I need to use the bathroom," I said, shifting uncomfortably in the backseat.

"We'll be home soon," Papa said, slowing the car as we drove through the town. He waved at Kip and Gladys, who worked at the Ketchum post office. I found it strange they were at work since they rarely opened on a Sunday.

I ground my teeth when Papa went over a bump, rocking the car. "Papa, please, can you stop? I need to use the bathroom."

"Toughen up, boy, we're almost home."

Tears welled in my eyes. Pain erupted in my tummy.

"Oh Jesus, fine, I'll stop at the gas station."

As Papa stopped the car, I bolted out, but I didn't make it

to the bathroom in time. I stopped a stone's throw away from the door that led to the men's bathroom. The warm urine ran down my leg, in my shoe, and absorbed into the dry sand.

"Oh shucks," Papa said beside me, "it looks like you didn't make it after all. You can be lucky you didn't do that in my car." He chuckled. "I would've beaten you so badly if you messed in my car."

"Jacob wet his pants. Jacob wet his pants," three boys sang as they passed us on their bicycles. They were from my class and I knew they would tease me at school tomorrow again.

My cheeks heated, and I covered my crotch area with my hands. I glanced up at Papa, who still grinned down at me.

"Come, you've already wet yourself. Might as well climb into the car like that." Papa climbed into his car and started the engine. He glanced over his shoulder, staring at me.

Heat rose into my chest, and neck and I fisted my little hands.

"Move it," he yelled.

I stomped toward the car, opened the door, and climbed inside, slamming the door closed. My cold, damp pants stuck to my skin, making me shiver. I folded my arms across my chest, and I didn't want to look at him.

"You will become a man one day and you need to stand up for yourself," Papa said, glancing at me in his rear-view mirror now and then while he drove. "And one of those things is managing your bladder. You can't go around pissing your pants."

"Yes, Papa," I said, glancing out of the window. Our farm was on the outskirts of Ketchum, a quiet mountain town far from any city, yet close enough that one didn't want to go anywhere. Mountains surrounded our town with crystal clear waterways, hiking, and biking trails, and when it snowed everybody went skiing.

"And you need to stand up to those boys," Papa said. "They're going to bully you."

I didn't want to talk to him anymore, so I continued glancing out of the window, watching the world go by.

We passed the local cemetery where they had buried Ernest Hemingway. Mama had told me a story about the famous author and how he killed himself. They diagnosed him with some disease I couldn't pronounce. His father, sister and brother also killed themselves; I hoped I didn't get what they had.

Papa turned onto the dirt road leading up to our farm-house and relief washed over me; I could take a nice bath and put on dry clothing. I wrinkled my nose at the smell of my urine-stained pants.

When Papa stopped the car, I climbed out and sprinted up the path toward the house, then stopped when Papa called me.

"Hurry, boy, you have chores to do."

"Yes, Papa," I said, climbing up the veranda stairs. When Papa was no longer looking at me, I bolted through the open front door, slamming it behind me. Then ran up the stairs to my bedroom and peeled the wet clothing from my body, throwing them in the laundry basket.

Hushed voices sounded outside my bedroom door, and then water started running in the bath.

There was a soft knock on my door. "Jacob," Mama said, slowly opening the door. "I've run your bath water."

"Thank you," I said, pulling off my damp underwear. "Sorry," I said, averting my eyes.

"It's ok, my son. Perhaps you should've gone before you left church."

"I wanted to, but Papa said to hurry."

She stared down at me with an expression I didn't understand. "Try harder next time because it will be difficult to clean your shoes." She picked up my soiled clothing and shoes and exited. "Hurry and bathe, your father needs you outside."

"Mama?"

She stopped and glanced over her shoulder. "What is it?"

"Why is Papa so hard on me?" I asked, my bottom lip trembling slightly.

Mama opened her mouth to say something but closed her mouth instead.

"Moira!" Papa yelled from downstairs. "Where's my boots?"

"In the closet near the front door."

"Now why did you move it there."

Mama rolled her eyes. "You left them there, Bill," she yelled.

"Don't talk back to me like that, woman."

"Yes, dear," she said, then turned back to me. "Honey," she started, then stopped as if there was something she wanted to say. "Never mind. Now hurry and be a good boy and go do your chores like Papa wants."

"Ok," I said and ran into the bathroom, slamming the door shut. I washed as quickly as possible, dried, and put on my work clothing. I didn't want Papa yelling at me again today.

The chore Papa had left for me to do was what I hated doing the most; to clean the chicken coop. But once that was done, I sat under my favorite oak tree that stood on a small hill a distance away from the farmhouse.

Papa's sheep roamed freely, grazing everything they could find.

I sat by the tree and watched the sunset. It was the first time this afternoon that I felt better after messing my pants. I felt safer and calmer out here.

Something moved out of the corner of my eye and I glanced in that direction. A wild hare sat staring at me. Slowly, I stood up and approached. The hare waited. I pounced. I caught the hare by its tail with my left hand and dug my fingernails into its body with my right hand.

I gritted my teeth as I applied more pressure. The hare made strange growling hissing sounds as it tried to get away. And I squeezed harder until bones broke.

Once I had secured the hare in my hands, I stood up. With one hand gripping it, I pulled the string out of my pocket and wrapped it around its neck. I tied the knot, ensuring the string was tight, and tied the other end of the string around a tree branch.

I watched the hare suffer while it died. There was something primitive yet satisfying about what I had done. I didn't understand it, only that I enjoyed it and wanted to do it again.

Grab your copy...
vinci-books.com/campbell1

About the Author

N. Gray is a USA Today Bestselling Author who lives in Cape Town, South Africa, with her daughter and adopted cat named Miss Beans. During the day, she's an analyst and provider profiler for a medical insurance company. At night, she types on her curved keyboard, creating fictional characters some may love and others you may want to kill yourself.

She writes in four genres: urban fantasy, thriller, horror, and paranormal romance.

She now writes under Natalie Michaels for her new thrillers and SD Syns for her new horrors.

Acknowledgments

Thank you to my dearest best friend, Angelique. You have been my ultimate fan, and I'm lucky to have you on my side.

Also, to my family: without you, I may not have gotten this far.

And to my editor. He has been awesome, to say the least. I'm sure he laughs at my South African slang, but he always gives me the right American terminology, and I'm grateful for his input.

Lastly, to my readers, thank you for reading!